ISBN: 978-1-915516-36-7

Rise of Dragons – Book 7

Eat, Pray, Dragons

G Clatworthy

Foreword

The idea for this book came to me after I saw something on the internet that proclaimed that adding the word 'dragons' to any title made it better. It started as a joke, but then Aloora whispered in my ear that this was her story and so I had to write it. I hope you enjoy this next instalment in the Rise of the Dragons series. This book is told from Aloora's point of view.

A special thank you to my amazing typo hunters, grammar gurus, and plot pickers who got this story to where it is today. You are awesome!

If you want to support Gemma, you can find her on www.patreon.com/G_Clatworthy for exclusive first reads of new stories. You can also join her newsletter at www.gemmaclatworthy.com for a free prequel to the Rise of Dragons series – and learn a little more about one of Aloora's exes – and follow Gemma on

www.instagram.com/gemmaclatworthy,

www.facebook.com/gemmaclatworthy or join the reader's group on Facebook: Gemma's book wyrms.

Chapter 1

I flung myself to the tiled floor to avoid the fireball, feeling the heat as it sizzled past my ear. Dzrak, that was close.

"How you holding up over here?" Dot, my vampire partner, asked, hauling me to my feet with ease.

"Still alive. But this dzraker needs to stop."

We'd been summoned when enough humans had reported a disembodied voice in a local rugby club's changing rooms on match days and the team had refused to play. The Magical Liaison Office got called in for these types of situations all the time. We were the front line in keeping the peace between supernaturals and mundane humans. Ninety per cent of the time, the calls were unfounded, and it was almost a full-time job sorting the fakes from the dangerous situations. But in this case, we couldn't ignore the volume of calls, and Agent Jones, my boss, had assigned me and Dot to investigate.

The club manager who greeted us thought it was a ghost and laughed it off as an overactive imagination, although his jaw was tense, and his brow prickled with sweat as he gave us the tour. A quick thermal body camera search – standard procedure in any haunting cases – had revealed a magic user had made himself invisible to perv on the players.

And he was powerful enough to launch fireballs while staying unseen. The dzraker. A prickling sensation, like pins and needles, ran up my arms. A sure sign that he was gathering magic. I might not wield power, but I could sense it. "Incoming!"

Dot ducked as a ball of flames landed where her head had been. She bared her fangs and ran forward, straight into another fireball.

Smart. The wizard was targeting the vampire and keeping her back. With her supernatural speed and keen senses, she was the bigger threat. I was a small gnome, barely five foot nothing on a good day, and without any advantages other than my Magical Liaison Office training and a keen thirst for learning. And I didn't think my researching skills would help today.

Dot shook her head and rubbed at her burned skin. She healed fast but vampires didn't like fire and she backed off, cornered by a volley of flame.

I caught her eye and whispered, "Distraction."

With her supernatural senses, Dot had no problem hearing me. She nodded back and set her lips into a hard line before reaching for her sword. It wasn't standard issue, but it was enchanted with ice power thanks to my best friend's sword-crafting skills and the vampire wielded it with force, spinning the blade so fast it was almost a shield against the onslaught of fire.

I wiped my brow. It was too hot in here. We'd locked the doors to trap him and now we were all in the same furnace. The pungent scent of sweaty feet mixed with the crackling smell of fresh fire. If we didn't end this soon, I might choke from the fumes.

Taking advantage of Dot's icy distraction, I crept around the locker room staying close to the walls. I kept my pace steady and slow, not wanting to make a sudden movement and draw the user's fire. My fingers gripped my standard issue crossbow, already loaded with a bolt of ash and silver. It was efficient; ash for fae, silver for most other supernaturals. Magic users like this one were typically immune to both, but that was why I had the crossbow. A couple of bolts with eighty pounds of kinetic energy behind it tended to neutralise most threats.

I eyed the fireballs, judging his location, and lined up my shot. I'd only get one before he realised I was here. A quick glance at Dot told me I needed to hurry up. Her pale skin blistered with heat, and she swiped her sword erratically. Her eyes glowed red. She needed to feed to speed up her healing, and it was never good to be the only visible source of blood in the room when a vampire went into a feeding frenzy.

Now or never.

I brought out the thermal imaging camera and aimed my crossbow at what I hoped was his shoulder. My finger curled on the trigger in a smooth motion. The bolt released.

The magic user screamed in pain and dropped his invisibility. Fantastic. He was naked.

I looked to Dot for help, but she shook her head and gave me a smile. "You shot him, you book him."

"You shot me!" The wizard was a bit behind current events. He blinked at his arm where the bolt had sunk in just above his elbow. There might be some muscle damage, but I'd avoided his vital organs, including the one pointing at me now.

I got out my magic cancelling cuffs and slapped them on his wrists.

"I'm going to sue! I've got rights, you know."

"Like the players you've been spying on have got rights?"

"You can't prove anything!" The wizard's eyes grew wide, and he yanked his arms away from me.

I sighed and started listing offences. "Trespassing, spying, misuse of magical powers to harm mundanes. I'm sure whatever you're up to is covered by the Sexual Offences Act, not to mention gross indecency."

"I don't know if I'd call it gross," Dot said, sauntering over. "It looks below average to me." She cocked her head to one side to better study his shrinking man parts.

"Hey!" The wizard turned his hips in a belated attempt to cover his deflating nudity.

Dot licked her lips, showing her pointed fangs. "I could use some blood to help me heal."

"She can't feed on me! That's not allowed." He looked to me with pleading eyes, as if I'd save him.

"Actually," I smiled, grabbing his upper arm just above the bolt so he winced, "vampires working for the Magical Liaison Office have the right to drink from apprehended suspects in extreme circumstances. Interestingly, they leave it up to officers' discretion to decide what counts as extreme. And I'd say getting torched by your magic counts as extreme to me."

The wizard sank in on himself.

"But I wouldn't drink from him, Dot. You don't know where he's been."

"I'm right here." The idiot didn't know when to shut up.

"Do you want her to bite you?" I asked.

The wizard shook his head.

Dot gave him a wink that made the wizard shrink even further. "It's alright, there's a blood pack in Dan."

We frogmarched the pervert to the van that Dot had insisted on naming Dan and sat him in the back.

Dot wrinkled her nose. "That's one of my homemade blankets."

"Do you want to throw out the blanket or the car seat?"

"Fair enough. I'll make another one." She downed one of the emergency blood packs we kept in a cooler in the van, pulled out some wool and a pair of knitting needles from the glovebox and started to create a new blanket. Her vampiric abilities meant she crafted at super speed. At this rate, she'd finish before we got back to headquarters.

I ran my hands over the steering wheel, inhaling the sweet scent of fuel combined with magic that made Dan the van run. "Ready?"

Dot looked over her shoulder at our prisoner, the needles in her hands never stopping. "Hold on tight."

With that warning, I accelerated, pulling the van out of the parking lot in a burst of speed. I loved driving. Adrenaline coursed through my blood as I weaved through the lanes, using the siren to skip red lights as if they didn't exist. This was freedom. This was exhilaration. This was… traffic.

I slammed on the brakes as we hit a queue I couldn't manoeuvre us around. I hated city driving. My fingers twitched. I longed for open roads, or the dirt tracks with tricky corners that I raced on at weekends. I huffed out a breath. Instead, I was stuck here.

We finally pulled up to the MLO headquarters after an hour stuck in mind-numbing traffic. I had to listen to the wizard bleat on about personal freedom and the constraints of clothing and how he was allergic to wool. Dot offered to hypnotise him into a sleeping state for the journey and he shut up sharpish. I shot her a grateful grin. I needed to think and plan how I was going to tell my best friend I was leaving the country in less than seven days.

"Schiztz," I swore in Dwarfish – the second-best language for swearing after Draconic – as we arrived at our destination. "I'm going to be late. Can you book him?"

Dot gave me a wave as she hauled the wizard into the office. "Give Dafydd a kiss from me."

Chapter 2

I took a sip of my peppermint tea and eyed the bundle in my friend's arms before my gaze wandered to her chest. Or, more accurately, her swollen bosom barely contained by her halter top.

It was fascination more than attraction that kept my eyes riveted on her breasts. Since giving birth, Amethyst's assets – always ample but now swollen to porn star proportions – threatened to break free from their restraints at the slightest movement. There must be a special branch of engineering specific to nursing mothers' clothes.

I drank some more of my tea, scanning the café for threats – an instinct I'd acquired from my job at the Magical Liaison Office. Rain pattered down on the windows in a typical Welsh summertime shower. Seeing nothing more threatening than a group of elderly ladies nattering, I coughed. "So…how is it?"

Amethyst looked up from her son with puzzled brown eyes. "It?"

I waved a hand. "Motherhood."

"Oh, yeah, it's…I don't know how to describe it. It's like the best thing that's happened to me. And I love Dafydd more than I thought possible…" she trailed off.

"But?" I prompted.

"But it's soooo hard. It never ends. Nappies and feeding and comforting. I've got no time to work on my jewellery business and I get these great ideas at three a.m. but then I forget them because I'm tired. The other day I fell asleep on the bus and went three stops past town centre. We almost ended up in Cathays." She shuddered. Cathays was one of the rougher parts of Cardiff, and a hotspot for student housing. There was probably a correlation between crime and academia somewhere. I used to live there in shared housing, but since moving to a nice place in the more upmarket Bay area, I hadn't gone back in years.

"You knew it was going to be like this, though? You took those classes."

Amethyst looked me dead in the eye. "Those classes did not prepare me for this."

I bit my lip, not sure what to say. I had done my research and had plenty of baby facts – did you know that a newborn baby has over three hundred bones? – but I didn't think that would help my friend.

She leaned forward, covered her baby's ears and whispered, "Sometimes, I think I'd prefer facing dragons."

I snorted a laugh at that. Amethyst had been present at the awakening of three dragons and several dragon attacks. I'd been there myself for most of them, but, unlike my best friend, I found the creatures fascinating, not terrifying.

"And Lorandir? Can't he help?"

Her face took on a dreamy look at the mention of her husband and I couldn't help my smile. On paper, a half dwarf and an elf shouldn't work, but he was besotted with her, and she loved him so much it made my heart swell to see my best friend so happy.

"He's a great dad…"

"But?"

"But his chest doesn't produce the milk that this chunky monkey guzzles." She pointed to her boobs, and I stared. Again.

"Speaking of…you're…" I gestured at her chest where dark patches spread over the fabric of her top.

"I know. They're dzraking enormous. It's embarrassing."

"No. You're…leaking."

"Schiztz. Not again. Can you hold Dafydd while I clean up?" Amethyst shoved her son into my arms and headed for the toilets.

I looked at the six-month-old in my arms. It was the first time I'd held him. I hadn't deliberately not held him, but it was easier to let others dote on the baby or leave him to sleep in his cot.

I swallowed, unsure how to cope with the small dependent person now in my arms. He was warm and heavy for something so small. Dafydd peered up at me with those big eyes, like he was so serious. I decided to treat him like he could understand me. "Did you know that you have over three hundred bones? An adult has two hundred and six."

He gurgled with interest.

"Maybe I'll make a scholar of you." I leaned in near his head and sniffed. Everyone said that babies smelled amazing. All I picked up on was sour milk and urine. "I love you because you're my best friend's son, but you do not smell great."

He burbled at me and clasped my necklace in his pudgy hands.

"You have good taste. Your mother made me this out of a dragon scale. It's the only one of its kind."

He cooed and pulled at the necklace, trying to bring it to his mouth.

"You'll have to try harder than that to get it off. It's dwarf made."

I prised his hands off my dragon scale. It was my favourite possession and as much as I loved my best friend and her baby, I did not want drool on it.

Outside, a car roared past as the driver over-revved its powerful v6 engine on the thirty-mile-an-hour road. What a waste of horsepower.

"Ahhh. What a cute baby." An older lady – in her sixties, perhaps – leaned in so close that I could see the lipstick smeared on her grey teeth.

"He is." It was a fact. The lucky baby had his dad's gorgeous elven features, but with Amethyst's big brown eyes so deep it looked like he could understand every word, and a thick mop of chestnut red hair that came from his dwarven heritage. He was going to break a lot of hearts when he was older.

"You must be so proud," the lady cooed before she made those strange babbles people make that they think the baby can understand.

I'd done research on that, too. It's critical for neurolinguistic development. But it's dzraking annoying to hear. "Why?"

"Why what?"

"Why would I be proud of him? He hasn't done anything remarkable." I knew. I'd compared him to standard progress markers, and he was entirely normal. I looked into his dark eyes and gave him the benefit of the doubt. "Yet."

The lady looked at me like I was speaking another language.

"Sorry. Did I slip into Elvish?" I spoke several languages fluently, but Elvish was the one I used most, after English. My jaw tightened. At least, I had spoken Elvish the most until recently, when my ex ended our five-year relationship and tossed me aside like a used notebook.

"No. You should be proud of him because he's your son." The woman was persistent, I'd give her that.

"Oh," I laughed, "he's not mine." Her jaw worked as she processed my words, probably deciding which authority to call to rescue the baby, so I quickly added, "He's my friend's."

"Oh. I bet holding him makes you want your own."

"Pardon?"

"Maternal instincts kicking in. It was the same with me. Once I held my niece, babies were all I could think about."

My instinct was to leave the conversation, but I was in the corner of the café and had nowhere to go, so I resorted to my lecturing voice. It worked on the students I had to tutor as part of my doctorate; maybe it would work on old ladies. Besides, I was already stressed from holding Dafydd, and the imposition of societal norms on me when I couldn't even make a relationship work was too much. I broke. "Not that it's any of your business, but I don't want kids."

"That's what you say now, but when you get older, you'll change your mind."

I stood and pulled myself up to my full height – five foot two with my boots on, so it wasn't impressive, but I was tall for a gnome – and looked her right in the eye. "I am thirty-nine and I think I know what I want in my life."

Her face reflected her shock. I looked young for my age. A combination of genetics, violet hair, and not having children interrupting my sleep.

"And furthermore–"

"Uh-oh," Amethyst breathed behind me. "So sorry. It took me a while to clean up, then I needed to pee. Looks like you made a friend. Hi, I'm Amethyst," she introduced herself to the interfering woman and took Dafydd from my arms.

The woman's jaw dropped. Seeing a real-life princess will do that. She mumbled something and backed away. When the woman reached her group of friends, she pointed back at us.

"You didn't have to step in. I had it under control." I said, sitting back down, the chair legs scraping on the wooden floor.

"Oh, I could see. You furthermore-d her."

"She was a busybody." I pursed my lips.

Amethyst chuckled. "You know you can win any argument, so why did you let some stranger rile you up?"

I sighed and picked at the sleeve of my skater-style dress. It was a delaying tactic, but I couldn't put off my news forever. "I'm going to Italy."

Chapter 3

"What? When? How? Why?" The questions exploded from my friend's mouth in an abrupt wave of punctuation that caused her son to cry out at the sudden lack of attention. Amethyst handed him a rubber chew toy in the shape of a giraffe without breaking eye contact with me.

"At the end of the month."

"And you didn't tell me?" Genuine hurt creased her eyes.

"You were busy."

"I'm never too busy for my best friend."

Guilt stabbed my chest. I could have told her when I decided over a month ago, but we saw each other so rarely since she'd had the baby that I didn't want to ruin the brief interactions we did get together by having the conversation we were in the middle of now.

People's priorities changed when they had kids. That was fine. Was I jealous of the attention that she slathered on her son? Maybe. Did I wish things could go back to how they were before when we lived together with Marco – the three musketeers? Perhaps.

But I also wanted her to be happy and if a baby was part of her choices, I would support my best friend. It just wasn't part of my plan.

"I didn't want you to worry." Maybe I should have just left and told her when I got back. She might have been too occupied with her family to notice I was gone. Even as I thought it, my heart winced in my chest. She was my best friend; I didn't want to run from her. But I had to go.

"Worry about what? You travelling by yourself to another country? Why would I worry about that?" Amethyst's voice rose as she babbled.

"I can take care of myself, you know." I was a bit put out that she saw me as some sort of bumbling academic, incapable of holding my own in the real world. I had a proper job with the Magical Liaison Office and had more combat training and mission experience than she did. I crossed my legs, feeling the weight of the knives in my boots. She didn't carry secret weapons.

Since having her baby, Amethyst hardly used her ancestral double-headed axe, although she had confided in me that she'd converted the buggy's undercarriage so she could store it there. Lorandir pretended not to know she took it out with the baby. It was a normal, healthy relationship. Not that I knew much about that – normal relationships, I mean.

Part of the reason I was leaving the country was because mine had broken down and I needed to escape seeing my ex everywhere. Not literally. She lived in the elven city of Breconia. But in little things, like my morning smoothie, which I still made double quantities of without thinking, or in the whisper of leaves on the breeze, or in the smell of old books which she carried with her from her job as a librarian. I sighed and drank more tea.

Amethyst leaned forward and placed her large, calloused hand over my ink-stained fingers. "I know you can. And I'm sorry you didn't feel you could tell me." She sat back. "I want to know everything."

I took a deep breath and drank more tea, allowing the earthy scent of peppermint to ground me. "Marco's going back home for the summer, and I'm going with him."

"So, you're not alone."

"Not for the first couple of weeks. He said I can stay at his family's house."

Amethyst's brow crinkled. "How long are you going for?"

"Three months."

"Three months!" She looked around and lowered her voice back to a normal speaking volume. "Sorry. But three months! What am I going to do without you? You're going to miss so much. Dafydd could be walking by then."

I raised an eyebrow at her as she held up her chunky son. "I'm pretty sure they have the internet in Italy. We can stay in touch. You can send me a video of his first steps."

"What else are you going to do while you're there, then?"

I couldn't stop the smile that crept across my face as I explained the real reason for my trip. "I found some texts in my research, and they reference this nunnery near Firenze." I rolled my tongue around the Italian city name, dzrak their language was gorgeous. "I've contacted the Abbess and they're letting me stay and giving me access to their archives. This is the last piece of the puzzle, Ame. I can finally finish my PhD."

My friend looked sceptical. I didn't blame her. I was a perpetual student who had changed my PhD topic so many times, even I'd lost count. But since freeing Fulgor, the blue dragon I counted as a close friend, and talking to him, I'd made so much progress understanding Draconic. I just needed a few more references – I couldn't exactly cite Fulgor as the source of all my research. And I also needed some peace and quiet away from the distractions of my job.

I loved working for the Magical Liaison Office, but I couldn't stick to standard office hours when rampaging chimeras were on the loose near Newport.

And I needed to get away from my ex. Putting over a thousand miles between me and Shesalva would give her the space she craved. Not that I was bitter.

"What did Agent Jones say?"

"She's fine," I lied. Agent Jones, my boss, hadn't been happy when I'd put in the request for the sabbatical, but Maxi had backed me up and offered to cover my role while I was gone. He still felt like he needed to make up for his part in raising a dragon years ago, but I wasn't too proud to take advantage of his offer.

I zoned back in to see my friend with her thinking face on.

"So…your doctorate relies on you going to a nunnery?"

"I know. It sounds like the start of a bad romance novel. But before you get excited, these nuns will probably all be ancient."

"But what if there's one who's younger?" She waggled her eyebrows at me.

"They'll be devoted to their God."

"I suppose you're with Shesalva, anyway." Amethyst sounded disappointed I wouldn't be ravaging any nuns while I was away.

I inhaled and put my cup down harder than I intended. Time to tell my best friend about my latest relationship failure. "Well…"

"What does that mean?"

"We sort of…broke up."

"You broke up and you didn't tell me?!"

"Again, you were busy. Baby." I pointed to her son, who had started to close his brown eyes, but opened them again at her outburst.

Amethyst stood and did a slow dance with a rocking motion designed to get him back to sleep. "What happened?" she asked in a quiet voice, singing her words to the tune of a soothing lullaby.

I shrugged, trying to play it cool. "She said she needed space to think about where we were going." I could tell Amethyst was about to take my side without knowing any of the facts, so I jumped in first. "It was my fault. You know me. I'm the lesbian they wrote the joke about; what does a lesbian bring on a second date?"

"A trailer full of her stuff."

"A U-Haul trailer," I stared at my friend. It was an American brand, but really? We had told that joke for years thanks to my tendency to fall head over heels for women who were totally inappropriate for me. I thought that had changed because Shesalva was perfect. I had to stop a sigh from leaving my lips. Not only was the elf gorgeous, but she also loved reading – like me – enjoyed long walks and sleeping in – like me – and she tolerated my love of dragons. But she'd made the decision that we didn't work, so here I was. Alone. Again.

"Baby brain. But you hadn't moved in together? Do not tell me that you moved in together without telling me!" Her rocking motion was now frenetic, but Dafydd had closed his eyes.

"No. Not exactly. She's an elf. They live for hundreds of years. We don't have the same concept of time. I thought I was playing it cool, but I might have mentioned that we could start looking for a place together. And…she freaked."

"She's an idiot."

I gave Amethyst a grateful smile. It was nice to have someone who was always on my side.

"She's not an idiot. She's the smartest person I know. That's the problem. She loves the library at Breconia. I love my job. She doesn't want to leave. I'll die centuries before she will. She said she needed space to think. So, I'm giving her space."

"Ally, I'm so sorry."

"Don't be." I forced a smile to cover my heartache. I knew what 'space to think' meant. I'd been dumped. Pulling myself back to the café, I lifted my cup, remembered it was empty and lowered it again.

"So, you're not running away?"

Dzrak, my best friend knew me well. I shook my head. "This is the kick up the bum I need to get this ruddy PhD dissertation finished, and, if I get to enjoy myself with some good food, great wine and fantastic weather in Italy…it's a hard life, but someone's got to do it."

"So, it's like an Eat, Pray, Love kind of thing?" Amethyst asked, placing Dafydd back in his pram before stepping back like he might explode. He cooed a little and rolled over but stayed sleeping.

"Did you actually read that?"

She waved her hand. "I saw someone talking about it online."

I shook my head with a wry smile. I had long ago given up on forcing my best friend to read anything other than fantasy novels.

"It's more like; eat, go to a nunnery, and study like crazy to get my dissertation done."

"That's a rubbish name for a book." My friend snorted and opened her mouth to say more but the lady from earlier was back asking for an autograph from the princess, aka my friend. I kept my mouth shut. Sometimes I felt like I was the only person in the world who could see that Amethyst didn't want the attention, but she wouldn't turn anyone away.

It was one of her best traits. I slipped to the toilets to avoid the confrontation I could feel bubbling under my skin – I wanted to tell the old lady to dzrak off and leave us alone. When I returned, the woman had brought her friends to coo at Dafydd. I contented myself with glaring at them until they left us alone.

Chapter 4

I folded my arms and glared up at the enormous blue dragon that towered over me. "It's not like that. I'm coming back."

I almost wished I hadn't told Fulgor that I was leaving for a summer in Italy. He hadn't taken it well.

"That is what you say, but you are small and may die away from me." Draconic was an expressive language and often had a touch of melodrama. I wasn't always sure that I understood him, but this was loud and clear; spoken directly into my mind.

I stepped up to Fulgor and stroked his blue scales. "I won't die. It's a trip to Italy, not a war zone."

"It is not safe for you to be so far from me."

I sighed. "I was alive and on my own in the world before you showed up."

"And I found you in a battle." He wasn't wrong. We had met during the battle for Avalon when he had been Mordred's mount, forced to do Mordred's bidding with a horrible saddle contraption that dug under his scales. I trailed a finger up a scar on his neck, my stomach clenching with anger at the ordeal this beautiful dragon had gone through.

"Where I rescued you," I reminded him, my voice a whisper.

He gave a snort and sparks of electricity shot from his nose before fizzling out. Fulgor was a sapphire lightning dragon, so unique that his powers weren't mentioned in any of the sources I'd read. And I'd read every book, scroll and parchment in the UK on dragons. That was another reason to go abroad, find some new texts, get my doctorate and have some space.

My gaze wandered to the tall trees of the elven city of Breconia. Shesalva was there somewhere. I could picture her moving along the elven treetop walks with grace, stacking books in the royal library with those perfect hands. I shook my head as if that could force the memories away.

She was the love of my life, or so I'd thought, until I'd ruined things by moving too fast. But I was pushing forty and gnomes didn't have the luxury of a centuries-long lifespan.

Fulgor picked up on the direction of my thoughts through our psychic connection. "So, this is about your mate."

I didn't understand why we could converse with our minds. My theory was that it had something to do with the trauma he'd suffered under Mordred and the dragon scale necklace I wore, and my fingers brushed its smooth surface. But I was grateful that we didn't have to have this conversation out loud.

"It's about my mate. My former mate," I said. There was no point trying to hide the truth from someone who could speak into your mind. "I need to leave. I can't be…here." I gestured around, but I didn't mean the nature reserve where we stood, or even the elven city adjacent to it. Everything about my life in Cardiff reminded me of her, so I had to leave. And I might as well use the impetus to finish my PhD and get something good out of it, instead of wandering the world like some lovesick lunatic, sighing over my broken heart. That wouldn't do anyone any good, least of all me. It was time to get a grip and move on. I had a lot to be thankful for; good friends, a great job, but staying here I got hung up on the one part of my life that was a disaster.

The enormous dragon inclined his head, his anger at me gone. "Love is a hard path."

I nodded. "Yep." I stared at the forest for another long minute before I turned back to the dragon. "What's your sob story?"

"Dragons do not sob." He made a noise in the back of his throat.

Draconic was a complicated language, full of contextual nuances, but it was also sometimes incredibly direct. "I meant, what's your love story? Dragons mate for life, don't they?"

Fulgor emitted a growling hiss. I tilted my head, picking up on the Draconic in its purest form. He had lost his love. And he was forced to remember it everyday thanks to the nesting dragons here in Breconia.

I laid a hand against his scales, each of them larger than my handspan, and we stood like that for a long while.

"Perhaps I should accompany you to this Italy," he said.

I considered the idea. It would be nice to have company, but the UK hadn't embraced dragons swooping overhead and Europe would be less welcoming. The EU might even take it as a declaration of war, even though Fulgor would never do anything to hurt anyone. Well, not on purpose. But dragons didn't know their own strength, and they had evolved into apex predators with ferocious cunning. I loved them, but not everyone felt the same way.

"Sorry, I don't think that's a good idea."

He huffed and lay down.

"I can call you, if you'll let any of my friends visit."

He huffed again.

I patted his nose, wincing as he let out a small spark of irritation. The psychic bond went both ways, and I could sense his annoyance. I turned to leave; this was not how I wanted our goodbye to go, but what did I expect? He was over a millennium old, recently freed from servitude to an evil despot, and now I was abandoning him.

"I have lived for centuries alone, a few weeks will be nothing," his voice came into my mind.

I smiled, whirled back, and hugged his massive snout. He let out a grumpy snort, but I could tell he was glad for the contact.

Parting on good terms put me in such a great mood that I forgot about the possibility I might encounter Shesalva.

Until I bumped into her. Literally.

Chapter 5

"Sorry," I mumbled, backing away from the gorgeous elf.

"The fault was mine," she said. Her voice was soft, like a whisper on the wind. The sort of voice I could listen to forever. "Why are you here?"

Heat spread through my face at the slight accusation in her tone, as if I had no right to be in this city.

"I wanted to say goodbye to Fulgor."

An emotion flicked across her face too quickly for me to identify. "I did not realise you were leaving."

"Yeah, well, I'm going to Italy for a few months to finish my doctorate."

"I am so happy for you." Her gaze focused on the mossy floor underfoot.

She couldn't even have the decency to look me in the eyes. Anger spread through my chest. She had no right to feel happy for me. This elf was the main reason behind my decision to leave.

I had laid everything bare for her, shared my heart and soul, offered her up every atom of my being. I was all in and I had told her so. Like a fool, I had thought she was in the same space as me, so I hadn't even thought I was being brave when I spoke about moving in together and how we might share our lives.

But instead of excitement about our future, I watched Shesalva retreat before me into her bland elven gaze, so good at hiding emotion. She told me that we had fun, but she wasn't sure it could work, that we needed space, that we needed a break.

I had tried to talk to her, tell her it wasn't as hopeless as it seemed, pointed to my best friend and her elven husband as proof that a relationship between species could work, would work.

But she laid out the facts for me, as cool as any researcher. She'd done her homework and could cite her sources. That's how I knew she was serious. And so, our relationship ended, with no great fanfare, but with hard evidence that we could never work, and I was an imbecile for thinking differently. It left me broken and bruised and Shesalva looking so unaffected it was unfair. But I suppose our time together had been nothing more than a bump in the road for the long-living elf.

So, no, she had no right to feel anything for me. But politeness dictated I answer her. "Thanks," I said, almost proud of myself at how normal I sounded.

Shesalva looked up then. Her bright eyes took my breath away, like they always did. She had the sort of eyes that made you feel they could see into your soul. "I hope you will be happy. It is all I want for you," she said.

I swallowed down the bitterness that filled my mouth. If she wanted me to be happy, why did she want this 'break'? And why call it a 'break'? Everyone knew that was just code for 'I want to break up with you'.

"I'm giving you the space that you wanted," I replied.

"I know that is what I said, but maybe we could talk. I…" Shesalva paused and took my hand. Her eyes filled with pain.

My anger returned. She had no right to feel upset. I was the one who had cried into my pillow every night for two weeks. I was the one who had consumed five litres of ice cream and too many chocolate bars to count. I was the one who had to struggle through her life as if her heart hadn't split in two.

I yanked my hand from her cool grasp. "Don't. Just…don't."

I walked away. Away from the beautiful elf who I had thought was my soul mate, away from the dragon I had bonded with and away from the peaceful elven city with its sweeping trees.

My phone beeped, and I pulled it out to find a message from one of my followers.

BigDragonEnergy: Your trip sounds amazing. I'll be in Italy too. Maybe we'll c each other. U can help me with Draconic datives.

At least someone was happy about my plans. I tapped out a reply, not wanting to alienate one of my biggest supporters, but I didn't need any distractions.

Aloora_Dragonquest: Thx. But won't have time to meet. Need to focus on thesis.

It was time for me to find myself without the ties I had to Wales and the people I loved here. It was time for me to go on a personal journey of discovery, eat my way through a dzrak-tonne of ice cream, and finish my dzraking thesis.

Chapter 6

I yawned and stretched as I sat on my suitcase in Rome's airport. Marco leaned against the wall next to us, phone out, designer sunglasses on, looking like he'd stepped out of a fashion magazine. It was criminal that he could look so good with so little sleep.

I, on the other hand, had bags under my eyes and travel hair. I knew. I had looked in the mirror in the bathroom.

Not for the first time, I wondered if this trip was the right thing to do. I was running away from everything in my life – my best friend and her new baby, my ex, my favourite dragon, my job – under the guise of doing something for myself. And a traitorous part of my mind whispered that under all of that, it was an excuse to keep running from my disastrous love life, or lack thereof, back home. But did it even matter if it pushed me to finish my thesis? The questions were too big for my sleep deprived brain to deal with right now, so I ignored them.

"My brother will be 'ere soon."

I nodded, welcoming the interruption into my thoughts, and clutched a shop-bought apple juice. The label claimed it was 'hand pressed' despite the fluorescent green colour. It did nothing to help my headache or my tiredness. An announcement said that the delayed eight thirty flight from Chicago had arrived.

Marco peered at me over his sunglasses. "When in Italy, you should drink coffee."

"You want me to get a coffee here?"

He sniffed. Marco did not approve of airport coffee. Or instant coffee. Or any coffee outside of Italy. I closed my eyes, shutting off the possibility of a lecture on how superior Italian coffee was. Maybe I could sleep on the hard floor if I used my satchel as a pillow.

A prickle ran down the back of my neck like someone watched me trying to doze. My eyes snapped open.

"Dragonquest!"

I searched the airport for whoever had shouted my name, but a crowd of people surged through the gates, blocking my view. On tiptoes, I looked for a familiar face through the horde of tourists and businesspeople in their crumpled suits. A chorus of car horns blared away any chance I had of finding them. Never mind. If they knew me, they could get in touch online.

"Lorenzo!"

I turned, swaying as my groggy body struggled to function on less than nine hours' sleep. I was not a morning person, and the flight had been at six a.m., which meant we had got to the airport for four in the morning, which meant getting up at two. It was hardly worth going to bed.

I focused on the tall man getting out of a battered eggshell blue Fiat 500. It looked like the Vegoia brothers shared the same poor taste in motor vehicles.

But they had the same good looks, too. His brother was a fraction shorter and his hair a little longer, but he still looked like a model and was far too cheery for this time in the morning.

He swept Marco into a hug and both of them launched into rapid Italian.

I stood to one side, waiting for their emotional greeting to finish, but he pulled me into an embrace and planted a wet kiss on one cheek, then the other.

"Signorina, my brother did not tell me you were so beautiful."

"Grazie."

"And you speak Italiano?"

"Si, un po'." It was a modest response. I was great at languages, already knew enough Italian to speak to Marco in his native tongue when we were alone in the apartment we shared, and I'd brushed up on the language ever since I'd decided to come. I was almost fluent.

Lorenzo beamed at me, grabbed my suitcase, and strode to the car like he was walking a runway.

I climbed into the car while he deposited my bag in the boot and frowned when I couldn't shut the dented door.

"You have to slam it," a woman's voice said.

I jumped. I hadn't noticed the beautiful woman in the back seat. A sign of just how tired I was, because I normally would have at least said hello as I appreciated her flawless skin and silky black hair.

She smiled at me while I stared, then leaned over and shut the door with so much force the car rocked.

"Giulia! What the hell? You want to break my car?" Lorenzo climbed in and slammed the driver's door even harder.

"Car? What car? This is a piece of crap."

I smiled at their Italian bickering.

Marco got in. "It is a piece of crap car," he agreed. I snorted. His car back home was worse than this – an ancient Volkswagen with a broken radio and no suspension.

"Forgive my brother and sister. They are rude to their big brother." Lorenzo turned to me and smiled. "No problems. We have music to block them out."

He pressed some buttons on the stereo, and Italian pop filled the car. He nodded his head in time with the beat and pulled out into the airport traffic without looking.

I gripped the 'oh-schiztz' handle and grinned as we sped through the lanes, hurtling into central Rome. Now this was a wake-up call. Adrenaline was so much better than caffeine.

Beside me, Giulia cursed her brother in rapid streams of Italian that I couldn't keep up with and I sank back against the scuffed leather seats and enjoyed her voice as it dripped pearls of vulgarity around me.

I loved languages of all kinds, from the rules of Latin and Dwarfish to the contextual subtleties of Draconic to the romance of modern French. And, in Giulia's mouth, Italian took on the same romantic glamour.

It was like hearing Latin's cool, younger cousin and I lapped it up, storing up the wonderful curses to add to my lexicon of swear words.

Dwarfish was still the best language for swearing – I mean, come on, don't tell me you can beat 'cocht-wimble' to describe someone who's being a complete arse – but I enjoyed the soft sounding Italian curse words.

They were almost a caress against the ears while telling someone to go dzrak themselves. It was the tone that told the recipient it was meant as an insult and not an erotic suggestion.

"Forgive my sister," Marco said, "she is no lady."

Giulia punched him on the arm and continued her tirade of insults; at her brother's driving, at Marco's scarf, at a taxi that got too close to the car. She was indiscriminate in her targets, but all of them got curated streams of insults that sang in my ears.

I smiled, and for the first time since leaving Wales, I knew that this was the right place for me to be. "Oh, I don't mind at all."

Chapter 7

Lorenzo pulled up outside a large house on the outskirts of Rome. The plaster on the building had faded to a warm, creamy yellow that set off the terracotta tiles and gave it a homey feel. A motorbike sat in the driveway and a large person bent over a toolbox on the concrete next to it.

The Vegoias got out of the car and Giulia walked around to help me wrestle the door open. She smiled as she offered me her hand and pulled me out of the piece of junk car.

A large woman with forearms that would make any bodybuilder proud, and a head of thick, glossy dark hair, stepped out from behind the bike. She shrugged off her overalls to reveal a floral dress that floated past her knees.

The woman wiped her oily hands on a rag and held her arms out before running over to us. "Marco! Bambino!"

"Mamma!"

Marco and his mother embraced while she peppered him with kisses. "Let me look at you." She pulled away, pushed back a lock of his black hair and stared at him with an intensity that I hadn't seen before.

Embarrassed by the show of familial affection, I coughed and shuffled in my canvas shoes.

"And your friend! Come here!" She kept Marco tucked under one arm and beckoned me over with the other.

"Buongiorno, Signora Vegoia," I said as I walked over.

Her smile broadened until it creased her entire face. She replied in Italian, "Welcome to my home," and pulled me into a hug so tight it squeezed the breath from my body.

There was something about Mamma Vegoia's embrace; it was warm and smothering in the best way. It pulled me in and leant me support and made me feel I was loved, even though I was a complete stranger to her. I leaned into her soft body and closed my eyes, squeezing back tears.

I felt like she accepted me just for being me, and that was priceless.

"We're here too, Mamma," Lorenzo said with a smile in his voice.

"Foolish child! I can see you any day of the week, you still live here with me. But they have come to see me from England!"

I bit back the correction on my tongue. Technically we lived in Wales, which was a different country, but I didn't want to ruin the bond with Mamma Vegoia with facts.

She loosened her arms and transferred one from my back to my waist. "Come, come, you must eat."

She ushered us all inside to the large family kitchen where a well-loved wooden table supported enough food to feed an army.

Mamma Vegoia pushed me into one of the mismatched chairs and handed me a plate. "Eat, eat, look at you, so skinny!" With a shake of her head, she piled fruit, bread, and cheese in front of me.

It all looked so vibrant and delicious. The strawberries were a darker red than I'd seen in the supermarkets in the UK and the sweetness as I bit into one overwhelmed my tastebuds. I glugged down fresh orange juice and followed it with a bite of ripe watermelon that dribbled down my chin.

I grinned as the others tucked in. This was family.

"So, tell me, bambina, do you have a man in your life? Lorenzo is unattached. He might look like an idiot, but his heart is in the right place, hmm?" Mamma Vegoia asked as she clattered around the kitchen brewing coffee.

Lorenzo winked at me, unabashed at his mother's matchmaking efforts.

I choked on my watermelon and coughed into a yellow napkin that Marco passed me.

"Mamma! Please! She has just arrived! And anyway, she prefers women," Marco said as he helped himself to the sliced ciabatta.

The older lady went silent for a few seconds, contemplating this revelation.

I tensed. Older generations weren't always understanding about people who didn't fit into typical social ideals, and I was both a supernatural and gay, so I didn't exactly fit. And, although I could argue about 'what's normal, anyway?', I didn't want to put that space between me and this loving family.

"No matter. He is no good for you anyway, too much lazing about, not enough helping his mamma in the kitchen!" She swatted a tea towel at his head.

Lorenzo laughed and carried on shovelling mini pastries onto his plate.

A cunning gleam crept into Mamma Vegoia's eyes. "Giulia, you will have to show Aloora the sights while she is here, yes?"

"I'd love to," Giulia said, giving me a smile.

"Thank you, that would be lovely." I couldn't help but feel like they had just set me up.

Chapter 8

In the Vegoia house, there was no time for naps, no matter how tired I was after the early flight.

Mamma wanted to know what my plans were while I was in Italy, so I told them, "A bit of sightseeing around Rome, and then off to the Sisters of San Silvestro near Firenze for some research."

"Yes, but what do you want to see in Rome?"

"The usual tourist things, I guess; the Colosseum, catacombs, the Vatican, maybe take a train down to Pompeii." I sounded casual, but I had done my research and had a list of all the places I wanted to check off.

"Not Pompeii," Mamma Vegoia said, "it is too touristy. Herculaneum is better. Giulia will take you."

"And you have to try the pizza here." Lorenzo scribbled down the name of a pizzeria. "It's in Naples. You can have it on the way back from Herculaneum." He leaned forward. "It is the best pizza in Italy and therefore, the world. You must order the margherita, that is all. It is the best." Lorenzo closed his eyes in pleasure.

"So, no ham and pineapple?" I joked.

Lorenzo's eyes shot open. "Pineapple on pizza?" He shuddered. "Blasphemy."

"You can go tomorrow," Mamma Vegoia decided.

"Mamma, please, Aloora has only just arrived. What if she wants to rest?" Giulia protested.

"Why would she want to rest when she has such short time here? No, she will stay here today and tomorrow, you will show her the sights."

That was decided then, and all without me having a choice. I finished my plate of sumptuous food and yawned.

Mamma Vegoia ruffled Marco's hair and told him to show me to my room. He led me over tiles the colour of Mamma's tanned skin to a cool room decorated with pages torn from fashion magazines and swatches of paints in a kaleidoscope of colours. Shutters kept out the dust and the heat.

"Your bedroom? Marco, I can't."

"It is only for a couple of weeks; I'll share with Lorenzo. Not a problem, as long as you let me escape in here when my brother decides to shave my head."

"He wouldn't?"

"He has a strange sense of humour sometimes." Marco rummaged in a drawer and pulled out a photo album that showed his younger self in denim dungarees and, yes, a shaved head.

"Come in whenever you need to."

"Grazie. Enjoy some rest. Mamma has a big meal planned for tonight. And when I say big, I mean gigantic."

"She's amazing. I've never felt so at home with anyone so fast."

A frown crossed Marco's face before he smiled. "She is good with people. I'll speak to her if you feel smothered."

"Not at all." I was quick to put him at ease. His family had taken me in and offered me a place to stay while I acclimatised to Italy and psyched myself up for the mammoth study session ahead. I didn't want to cause any ruptures between them. "It's all good. It's refreshing to have people who accept me for who I am."

I hadn't spoken to my own family, with the exception of my eccentric uncle, since I'd come out. My parents weren't exactly modern and the thought that I preferred women to men was a concept they found hard to accept. Their rejection still stung, but the pain in my heart had dulled with time. I had other friends now – my found family – it was just a shame that their lives moved on while I was a perpetual student and perpetually doomed to fail at relationships and perpetually fighting ignorant views on dragon rights in my job.

With a sigh, I sank onto the crisp bedcovers and closed my eyes. Everything would feel better after some sleep.

Unfortunately for me, Mamma Vegoia's idea of a restful day involved what seemed like every single relative they had in the whole of Italy dropping in to see Marco and me. Every time I closed my eyes, a new aunt or uncle or cousin arrived, and Marco came to get me with a sheepish grin. Apparently, I was considered part of the family and had to greet everyone.

By mid-afternoon, I'd even accepted the offer of coffee to get me through the day. The bitter drink was hard to gulp down, but it kept me awake. I downed three cups before Giulia took the mug from my hands.

"Best to stop when you start shaking."

I looked at my trembling fingers; a small price to pay to help me stay awake and not snap at the good-natured Vegoias who all embraced me with a kiss on each cheek as they presented me with chocolates and sweet treats.

There was no way I could stay on a healthy diet in this country, so I gave in, and sent pictures of every pastry to Amethyst who responded with drool emojis that made me laugh.

I streamed a short video to my Dragonquest social media channel about living the vita dell'Italia and spouting some of the dragon lore I had researched before leaving England, which got a lot of likes as I talked.

Mamma Vegoia walked in at the end of the shot and became an instant hit with my followers when she called me too skinny. I laughed and ended the stream.

"You did not say your research was on dragons," she said, sitting down next to me on the bed.

"I'm interested in their behaviours but the language most of all, it's fascinating."

"You should be careful, bambina, the saints put dragons to sleep for good reason."

"I know," I sighed. The proclivity of so-called holy people or knights killing 'evil' dragons was a staple of Western mythology.

"Why do you sound so sad?"

"Dragons are amazing creatures, so wise and beautiful, and I wish people could see them as I do. We've had dragons in the UK for a few years now and they don't kill anyone. They just want to live like any other species."

"Did you know there are legends that dragons still slumber here in Italy, too?"

I leaned forward. That hadn't come up in any of my research.

"It's true. They say that some dragons were buried and simply sleep. Perhaps that is why Vesuvius still smokes." Mamma Vegoia laughed.

My lips curved. Her joy was infectious.

"Now, come, you will eat."

Chapter 9

We sat outside in the warm summer evening. I pinched my thighs under the table to keep myself awake as Mamma Vegoia served Parma ham with fresh juicy melon slices from fruit she'd harvested earlier in the day. The Vegoia garden was a haven of tranquillity, with lush vegetation climbing the walls. A huge tree sprawled above us, making the garden feel cosy and absorbing the noise of the city, so it felt a long way away, almost like we were in another, more peaceful, time.

A rustle of leaves had me looking up just in time to see a scaled creature fly at my face. I yelped and dodged. Thanks to my MLO training, my reaction times were fast, and the creature landed on the paved ground behind me. I stood, flinging my chair back, ready to fight. A couple of people snickered from the table. My heart pounded before my brain kicked in. It must be a wyrm – a dragonlike creature that people sometimes kept as pets despite their proclivity for setting things on fire – Amethyst had one that helped in her jewellery forge.

The creature regained its balance and jumped up into my lap, placing its front legs on my shoulder as it studied me. None of the Vegoias reacted with more than veiled amusement, so I took it that this little wyrm wasn't a threat. It didn't have any back legs and, now that I wasn't worried about an attack, I could see that it wasn't a wyrm at all; its body was too thin, and its wings were smaller, suitable for gliding through treetops.

"A jaculus," I breathed. "I thought they were extinct."

Seen as a threat during Roman times, they'd been hunted to the brink of extinction thanks to their tendency to ambush passersby from the trees and knock them to the ground with enough force to render people unconscious. The ancient writers were sketchy on whether they'd eaten their victims or not. Looking into the intelligent creature's eyes as he studied me, I'd wager they did it out of mischief rather than malice.

"Giacomo, get down." Giulia picked the winged serpent from my chest and plonked him on the floor.

"Aiee! What is that naughty snake doing now? Can't he leave our guest alone?" Mamma Vegoia rushed from the doorway holding an enormous dish of salmon and vegetables, which she handed to Marco before planting her hands on her hips.

"He's just saying hello, mamma." Giulia tickled the jaculus' neck, and the snake wiggled with delight, flicking out his forked tongue.

"It's no problem," I said. "I was surprised. We don't have them in the UK."

"We shouldn't have him here, but he won't leave." Mamma Vegoia glared at the serpent. The jaculus wound himself around Giulia's neck and shot her a triumphant look. Mamma Vegoia threw up her hands in despair as if this was a conversation they'd had many times before. "I suppose we must live with the relic of ancient times."

Giulia sat down. Mamma Vegoia's nostrils flared. "Not at the table! How many times must I say it?"

Giulia unwound the snake and popped him on the ground, slipping him a leftover piece of Parma ham. She shot me a wink that had my lips curving into a smile. Giacomo made his way back to the tree, using his front legs to crawl forward while his long tail curved behind him in a twisting 's' motion. He clambered up and perched on a branch overhanging the table, his keen eyes on the food.

I was definitely awake now.

Chapter 10

The next morning, I struggled to consciousness as someone knocked on the door.

"Five more minutes." I rolled over, pulling the thin covers with me.

"You must get up if you are to eat before going to Napoli."

"I'll skip breakfast," I said.

Mamma Vegoia's earthy laugh boomed through the door as if I'd told a great joke.

Marco entered with the casual ease that came from sharing a flat together back home. He looked far too good for this early in the morning.

"What time is it?" I mumbled.

"Eight o'clock."

"Dzrak off."

Marco laughed, used to my poor behaviour in the mornings. "You should get up or Mamma will come in and make you."

"Fine. I'm getting up. Happy?"

"I'll be in the kitchen." He snatched a chequered scarf from a drawer and left me alone.

I considered burrowing back under the covers, but the thought of Mamma pulling me from the bed stopped me. Instead, I pulled on some clothes, brushed my hair and took groggy steps to the kitchen.

I had got to bed late last night while the Vegoia clan drank their coffees and joked together, unaffected by the late hour. And this morning, the entire family sat smiling brightly in the kitchen. Who were these people that they could function with less than seven hours of sleep?

I sank into a hard chair and poured myself a glass of juice. If these were the hours that Italians kept, no wonder they were so obsessed with coffee.

It was tempting to give in and help myself to some of the black elixir that bubbled in a glass jug, but I preferred natural ways to wake me up, so I stuck with the sweet orange juice.

Outside, Giacomo scrabbled at the door, begging to be let in. I stood, but Giulia told me to ignore him. The jaculus wasn't allowed in the house or he'd set up on the top of the cupboards and jump down at Mamma while she cooked.

Mamma Vegoia pursed her lips. "He is a nuisance."

"You love him really, mamma," Marco said, brushing a comb through his hair and making himself look more like a model than ever. It wasn't fair.

Mamma Vegoia ignored him and pushed a plate of sliced bread and crumbling pastries towards me. "Eat, eat."

"I'm not hungry, honest." I held up my hands in protest. I needed sleep, not calories.

She pursed her lips again, about to scold me for missing a meal when Giulia intervened. "We'll take some with us, Mamma. Come, we'd better go, or we'll miss the train." She stood and tapped Lorenzo on the shoulder. "Come on, you're our lift to the station."

"What if I had plans?" he grumbled as he drank his coffee down and tucked a paper under his arm.

"Like a job?" Giulia asked with a wink.

Mamma took a deep breath, and Lorenzo rushed from the kitchen. With a smile, Giulia grabbed two pastries and left the room. I downed the rest of my juice and followed.

"Thanks," I said once we were outside.

"No problem. Mamma can be funny about food."

She handed me my pastry, and I bit into it. It wasn't my usual healthy smoothie, but the flaking buttery pastry and sweet sugary taste were divine.

"Don't get crumbs in my car," Lorenzo said as we slammed the doors shut.

Giulia took a slow, deliberate bite, crumbs tumbling from her full mouth.

I laughed and sprayed pieces of the dry pastry everywhere.

Cursing, Lorenzo pulled out and headed for the train station. As much as I wanted to nap on the way into Rome, Lorenzo's driving was so erratic that I couldn't rest my head against the door without banging it as he swerved across lanes. After his third tight turn, adrenaline coursed through my veins as my body didn't know if it would survive the dash through early morning traffic. It was better than coffee.

My fingers itched to take the wheel. Driving in the UK was so constraining. The roads were so boring, and everyone had respect for the speed limits. Here, it was chaos.

Too soon, Lorenzo pulled up in a no-parking zone and told us to get out while he stared down a polizia in a dark uniform who walked towards the car.

We jumped out, and he sped off just as the police officer got within ten paces. The guard glared at us but returned to his post.

Giulia laughed and bought us tickets before steering me to a coffee bar.

"I don't drink coffee." Not unless I had to stay awake to greet Italian nonnas.

"When in Rome…" she replied with a smile. "But I think you should try this instead." She ordered two chocolates.

In my experience, any food or drink you bought at a railway station was about a hundred times worse than the regular stuff, so my expectations were low when the barista placed two small cups of hot chocolate in front of us. I sniffed it cautiously. The aroma of rich chocolate had me drooling, and I stirred the dark drink. It was so thick; it felt like stirring a mousse.

Giulia gave me a knowing grin and scooped a spoonful into her mouth like it was a dessert. I followed suit and moaned in pleasure. It was perfect.

I took a picture and sent it to my channel.

Giulia watched me with curious eyes. "Why do you do that?"

"Do what?" I asked as I added a caption and sent off another personalised text to Amethyst.

She sent me a picture of what I hoped was Dafydd's breakfast; mashed up cereal and milk. Very unappetising.

"Feel the need to put everything about your life online?"

"I have to. My followers know about my trip to Italy. They expect updates. And I don't share everything about my life, just the stuff related to dragons."

"Why dragons?" It was almost the same question that her mother had asked me yesterday.

"Because they're fascinating, and we know so little about them. I want to understand more. I want to know everything there is to know about them. That's why my handle is Dragonquest. This is my purpose."

"Is it?"

It was an innocent question, so why did it feel like it cut into my soul?

I did the mature thing and drank instead of replying. Giulia gave me an enigmatic smile worthy of the Mona Lisa and tapped me lightly on the arm. "Come, we have a train to catch."

It was just over an hour to Naples on the train, so I closed my eyes as the sumptuous Italian countryside zipped by and caught up on some much-needed sleep.

I awoke to Giulia's gentle hand on my shoulder. "We're here."

She led the way to another platform where we caught a short train to Herculaneum, the less well-known town that was destroyed by the same famous eruption that coated Pompeii in ash.

We decided to tour the archaeological site first, then come back and walk round the museum before having pizza at the place Lorenzo had recommended. He had told us the name again in the car just to make sure that we knew where we should go. If the expression on his face when he said the name was anything to go by, I was expecting an orgasm as soon as we walked in the door.

But, for now, we had an hour train ride to Herculaneum. I passed the time by making a montage video for my channel while Giulia was content to watch the scenery pass by. It was uncanny. I had never met anyone who was happy to live life and not stream it. Her phone never left the small black shoulder bag at her side once during the train journey, while mine beeped every minute with notifications.

Dr4gonista: Have fun in Pompeii

BigDragonEnergy: Pompeii! Fun. Maybe c u there

I was about to scribble a reply that I wasn't in Pompeii when we arrived at the Ercolano Stavi station and Giulia pulled me off the train into the mid-morning heat.

Chapter 11

It was a short walk from the station to the archaeological site, and there were a handful of tourists who followed the same route. You could tell the foreigners from a mile away. It was like there was a checklist: skin either pasty pale or burned red, backpack with water bottles dangling from the side, large hats, sandals, constantly checking signposts and phones for maps.

I fit right in with that description, despite my lack of hat or sandals. A decision I regretted as the sun beat down on me. Giulia was unaffected by the heat, tilting her face up to the sun like it nourished her.

I slathered on a generous amount of sun cream as we walked, trying to protect my skin. Gnomes were an indoor people, and we didn't do well in the heat, preferring libraries and workshops to the great outdoors and the pitfalls of nature, although I made an exception when visiting dragons.

Vesuvius loomed in the background, looking like an innocent mountain. It was hard to believe something so peaceful could have destroyed two prominent Roman towns one unremarkable October day in the first century.

"Some people say it was not a volcano at all, but a huge dragon that the locals angered," Giulia whispered conspiratorially.

"Why did it stop, then? Why not destroy everything?" I puffed up, ready to argue and pick apart the claims that a dragon had caused the natural disaster.

She shrugged. "Perhaps someone appeased it. A human sacrifice, maybe."

I clamped my lips shut. Every disaster seemed to have the rumour of dragon destruction behind it. It wasn't fair how these amazing creatures were victimised and blamed for anything bad that happened in human history, even while they were asleep. And, of course, the evil beasts would want a human sacrifice. Never mind that they were more than capable of hunting for their own food and that they found cows and horses tastier than tiny humans. In everyone's minds, dragons were demons.

My bad mood dissipated as we bought our tickets and took an audio guide to the site. The empty structures waited to be discovered, laid out like a gateway to another time. The possibility of learning something new tempted me to it, distracting me from my dark musings about the abuse of dragons in Western literary tradition.

A group gathered to one side. Tours were interesting but too structured for my liking; they didn't give enough opportunities for me to follow my curiosity and I could already tell that I would want to explore these ruins more fully than a guide would allow. I motioned to Giulia, and we sidestepped the tour to wander by ourselves.

The site was smaller than Pompeii, the more famous town, but if Pompeii was the large ugly sister, forever thrust upon tourists like a hefty suitor, Herculaneum was the forgotten but more beautiful Cinderella.

The audio guide informed me that it had been a wealthier town than Pompeii and the empty structures reinforced the message. I paused in a patch of shade on the largest street and imagined what it might have looked like in its heyday.

Large buildings lined the street – former houses, maybe a bath house, temples – hiding rich frescos and mosaics from prying eyes. The remains of paintings still stained the walls in ochre red and faded lines.

It would have been somewhere to see and be seen. I stepped forward and followed the street until I came to a large doorway flanked by orange pillars. The House of the Great Portal, according to the guide.

I peered inside, and a small dragon etched in a stone caught my eye. I snapped a picture and uploaded it. My followers would love this. Could the Great Portal hold an entrance to another world?

There was a dim residual magic around, but I couldn't pick up more than that. Gnomes were better able to tune into magical texts and artefacts. I theorised that it was an example of self-defence evolution in action. If you tinkered with something, it was good to at least know if you had a chance of blowing yourself to smithereens.

"The real treasures were taken to the museum," Giulia said, interrupting my thoughts.

"Smile for the camera," I said and took her picture.

She smiled, and I stared. Giulia looked so…right…here in a forgotten time. I took her in for a long moment before her look turned to puzzled and I took another picture, flushing at the sudden heat that crept through my body.

"My turn," she said and got her phone out of her handbag for the first time on this trip. She took a picture of the both of us and showed it to me.

"Great, share it with me and I'll put it online."

She shook her head. "Some things are better if they are not shared too far. This is just for us. Promise?"

It was a novel idea not to share my life on the internet, especially if it related to dragons, but all of that mattered less now I was here. It was the quest for knowledge itself that tingled through my skin, not the need to share it with others that had driven my growing social media channels.

I nodded. "Just for us."

She shared it with me then and I grinned like an idiot as the picture of the two of us came up on my phone. I looked relaxed and happy in a way that I hadn't seen myself for years. Maybe la magia dell'Italia was real…

Giulia pulled me away from the door and to another house with a colourful painting of a naked couple on the wall. She didn't comment as I took another picture and put this one online. Habits were hard to break, and my followers wanted updates.

Sometimes I felt like they were newly hatched baby dragonlets, and I was their mama, coughing up nuggets of dragon knowledge to feed their hungry mouths.

But in between the pictures and the posting, it was nice to just…be.

Giulia and I wandered through the abandoned town, admiring the columns and exposed hypocausts as the shadows shortened.

I wanted to see the House of the Papyrii, where one of the largest private ancient libraries had stayed buried for over nineteen hundred years. So much knowledge in one place. I almost expected to find forgotten scrolls there, even though that was ridiculous – everything had been removed for study years ago.

When we got to the house, the inside was closed for conservation so I could only marvel at the scale of it from the outside and peek at the colourful frescos within through the gaps in the masonry.

It was hard to believe that the same paintings I saw now were once viewed by ancient Romans every day and that the colours were even more vibrant back then.

I voiced my amazement to Giulia, who smiled and shrugged like she was used to living with history, and we moved on to the less upscale part of the town.

The boat houses sat like open tombs and chilled me to my soul. The audio guide told me that archaeologists had found almost three hundred skeletons – mostly women and children – huddled together as they tried to shelter from the pyroclastic flow that killed them.

I shivered despite the summer heat and moved away without taking a picture. It was too horrible to imagine the fear and pain they had gone through as they burned alive from the extreme heat of the volcanic eruption in a space they couldn't escape.

My palms grew sweaty as I thought about suffocating in this enclosed space – my worst nightmare. I couldn't even make it through a trip to the spacious dwarf mines in Wales without using alcohol as a crutch. If I'd been trapped here, I would have clawed the walls until my fingers bled.

Giulia took my hand and rubbed her thumb along my knuckles, bringing me back to the present and soothing my panicking mind. She knew exactly what I needed, and I was grateful for her quiet understanding.

As we moved back into the main streets, my mood lightened, and I finished our tour with a quick video for my followers, where I shared the rumours about the slumbering dragon in Vesuvius. Comments popped up, asking me to go there and investigate. It was tempting. I looked up at Giulia who leaned over a railing, surveying the ruins in the mid-afternoon sun, and decided against it. Vesuvius was a volcano, not a dragon, and maybe there were more important things than an online presence.

I didn't have much time to ponder this strange revelation because Giulia led me back to the train station for Naples and the museum.

61

Chapter 12

We grabbed some panini for a late lunch – pesto and prosciutto for me, tomato and mozzarella for Giulia – and headed through the Neapolitan streets to the large museum that held all the treasures taken from Herculaneum and Pompeii.

As we walked, I pointed out the piles of rubbish that lined the roads. Black bin bags perched precariously on top of one another, and old food and serviettes littered the streets, pouring out from tears in the lower strata of rubbish bags.

"There is a strike," Giulia said as if that explained everything.

As we picked our way past an overflowing public bin, she elaborated that the waste collection workers wanted more money to offset the rise in the cost of living.

"But this is nothing. You should have seen it years ago when there was the big problem."

I tried to imagine it.

"The streets were filled with so much rubbish, you couldn't walk in them. But that's what happens when the local government is inept, and the mafia is involved." She shook her head, causing her dark hair to move in hypnotising waves.

"What happened?"

She shrugged one shoulder. "Politics."

That was all I could get out of her on the subject before a scooter almost ran me over as we crossed the road to the museum.

The National Archaeological Museum of Naples was a vast building with a façade that looked like a Southern American mansion, complete with palm trees outside. Its pale pink plaster finish gave a sense of warmth in the midday sun. We stepped inside and I let out a sigh of relief as the air con washed over me.

We bought our tickets and walked through the rooms. There were too many statues to count of Roman and Greek mythological figures in various poses and states of undress among the rooms full of bright frescos, some incomplete, others almost perfect.

I pictured these works of art in the shells of the houses we'd seen earlier that day and felt both sad that they couldn't have stayed in their original location and happy that they were saved from looting and preserved here where we could gawp at them along with all the other tourists who pushed past us.

Giulia drew me to one side with a wicked grin and pointed to a sign that said 'Gabinetto Secreto'.

"The secret cabinet?" I asked.

She drew me inside and laughed as my eyes widened into saucers. This room was filled with anything the curators had thought was erotic.

I didn't have a lot of experience with penises – penii? No, that was ridiculous. Penes would be the correct Latin plural. If I was getting declensions wrong, I must be distracted – but I was sure some of those positions weren't possible and, if they were…ouch.

We walked past phalluses and paintings of orgies and a statue of Pan copulating with a goat. I took some pictures and sent them to Amethyst, imagining her blush at the erotic scenes.

I wasn't disappointed. My friend messaged back saying that she was at tea with her mother. I burst out laughing and a museum guard shot me a look.

Stifling my giggles, I sent more pictures and accidentally posted one online too, which drew a lot of responses from my followers. I declined to reply to some of the more…suggestive comments.

We moved back into the main part of the museum, and I took pictures of a small dragon mosaic and a jug with the handle modelled into a winged serpent.

The trouble with roman mythology was that there were so many ways of depicting snakes that it was hard to know if something was meant to be the winged staff of Asclepius or a stylised dragon or even a jaculus. But everything could be a clue to when exactly dragons had disappeared from the world.

Not even the ancient dwarven or elven texts could agree, and that was a big part of why I was in Italy, even if these first two weeks were technically a holiday. If I could find that out, I'd be at the cutting edge of dragon research, not that it was a competitive field; I was already the lead researcher in the UK because I always wanted to know more.

After we'd exhausted the museum and posed for pictures with some of the more underdressed statues, Giulia declared it was time for pizza.

Chapter 13

We paused outside an unassuming building painted white with a small sign hanging above the door. I checked the address again. This was it. A tiny plaque on the wall proclaimed that pizza had been invented here. I snapped a picture for my social media followers and went inside.

A cavernous pizza oven occupied a large portion of the restaurant, and the owner had crammed six tables into the rest of the small space. Not a single one of them had anyone sitting at them.

"Are you sure this is it?" I whispered to Giulia in English. I had expected crowds of people in the restaurant with the best pizza in Italy.

She nodded and pressed the silver bell on the small desk near the back. "We are early."

It was a fair point. It was six thirty in the evening, and no one in Italy ate before eight o'clock.

A small man with grey hair appeared. He exchanged rapid Italian with Giulia and led us to a table at the back of the restaurant. He asked us what we'd like to drink and returned with water and wine for us both.

We ordered two margherita pizzas, and he nodded with all the wisdom of a sage. He shouted something and a younger man entered wearing chef's whites. The newcomer rolled up his sleeves and fired up the oven before turning his attention to the dough.

Oblivious to us, he kneaded and pounded and spun the elastic dough into huge rounds as big as the wheels on Lorenzo's Fiat 500. He sprinkled on the toppings with practiced ease and shovelled them into the oven with a long wooden pizza paddle that looked older than the building.

The smell of cooking pizza wafted over to us, all bread and cheese and tomato. My mouth watered, and I took a sip of my wine.

"Why are you really here?" Giulia asked, fixing me with her dark gaze.

"To study. Marco offered me a place to stay first, so I thought I'd do some of the tourist things before hunkering down at the nunnery and finishing my dissertation."

"That is what you will do. I asked why you were here."

I drank more wine, letting the rich red fill my mouth with its fruity dark taste before swallowing. This woman was perceptive, and I weighed up what I wanted to say.

"I…wanted to get away," I said. Giulia stayed silent and words tumbled from my lips. "Everyone in my life is moving on, except me. I'm stuck. I haven't even finished my PhD, and it's been years. I've changed topics more times than Marco changes his sunglasses. It's like I can't move forward. So, if I can take some time away from all the distractions at home, I can finally complete it and achieve my dream."

"Becoming a doctor is your dream?"

I opened my mouth to say 'yes, of course,' but, instead I said, "Maybe. I don't know anymore."

That was more than I had expected. I gazed at the deep red wine in the glass. The Romans were onto something: in vino veritas.

Giulia nodded, wisdom beyond her years settling on her face. "It is alright to change your dreams. We are not who we were at twenty. We learn and we grow. That is life."

"How did you get so wise?"

"It's in the blood." She shrugged.

I leaned forward to follow up on that strange comment when our pizzas arrived. The aroma was a hundred times more intense when it was directly in front of us. The chef had torn up some basil and sprinkled it on top of the bubbling cheese, lending an air of freshness to the divine scent of tomato and mozzarella.

For a few seconds, I just stared at it. It was perfect. The pizza of pizzas. I took up my knife and fork and cut a small piece out of the circle.

As soon as it touched my tongue, I knew what heaven tasted like; creamy mozzarella, rich tomato sauce, fresh basil and comforting crisp yet fluffy dough. How could something so simple taste so good? I had eaten cheese pizzas before, but it was blasphemous to consider those in the same food group as the taste sensation that flooded my mouth.

I groaned with pleasure. "This is the best thing I have ever eaten."

Giulia's musical laugh rang through the air. As we sat and ate, the restaurant gradually got busier, with people coming in for their evening meals or to take away pizzas in branded cardboard boxes.

The owner was unhurried with every customer, chatting with regulars, recommending toppings and wine, while the chef made the pizzas to order, each one a sensual experience of throwing dough, scattering semolina flour and choosing a careful selection of toppings. It was poetic to watch, so we did.

Giulia and I sat and ate and watched for the rest of the evening, only leaving at the last possible moment to make sure we made the last train back to Rome.

Chapter 14

The next day, Mamma Vegoia mercifully let me sleep in – Giulia and I had topped the evening off with wine back in the garden while Giacomo wound his way around my ankles, and had got to bed late even by Italian standards – and I woke to the sound of doors slamming as Marco's family left for whatever errands they had.

Yawning, I stumbled to the kitchen and poured a glass of juice before helping myself to some toast.

Mamma bustled in with a pile of clothes that she started to fold.

"Should I move?" I asked.

She waved away my suggestion and worked around me, but not before placing some rich crumbly pastries on my plate. "So, you had a good time with Giulia yesterday?"

I nodded a bit too eagerly. "She's great and Herculaneum was so interesting, and I need to thank Lorenzo for the pizza recommendation."

"Good, good. And today? You have plans?"

"Maybe the Colosseum."

"And you take food with you." It wasn't a question. Mamma Vegoia finished folding the washing and moved on to making me a baguette sandwich.

I muttered a thank you and retreated to my room to finish getting ready. I changed out of my pyjamas – a custom set made with a dragon print I'd found online – and into a dress. I debated leggings, but the weather forecast was for sunshine and heat, so I used a layer of sun cream instead before pulling on my canvas trainers and grabbing my satchel. A flick of eyeliner and I was ready.

Mamma handed me a bag bulging with food when I was less than two steps outside of my bedroom door.

"Thank you."

"It is nothing. Do you want Lorenzo to drive you? He does nothing all day but stay in his room looking at his computer." She raised her voice on the last sentence.

"I'm working, Mamma!" came the reply from behind a closed door.

"Working! You need a job to work! So, you want him to take you in?"

"No thanks, I'll get the bus."

Mamma Vegoia frowned, but I squeezed past her and made it to the front door. I gave her a wave and headed outside.

The late morning heat hit me like a tsunami of sunshine, and I blinked several times to get my bearings after the cool shade inside the house.

I pulled out my phone and walked to the bus stop where I leaned against the glass and did a quick post for my channel. After that, I went through the food bag.

Mamma Vegoia had packed me a huge sandwich so full of salami that it might give me a heart attack just looking at it. There was an enormous round tomato that I guessed I could eat like an apple, a packet of biscuits sprinkled with sugar, and a bottle of water. I had a drink, transferred it all into my satchel, and forced the buckles shut.

The dragon etched onto the leather front bulged out, but this bag had carried much heavier loads than a picnic; I regularly used it to tote home chunky library books from the university.

I messaged Amethyst. *I think I've eaten more food since arriving here than I normally do in a week!*

Her reply came fast. *Lucky! Enjoy it! I wish I could nom on Italian chocolate, and eclairs and pasta.*

Eclairs are French. And my body's a temple.

So, honour it with offerings of Italian goodness.

She attached a picture of Dafydd chewing on a rusk. Gooey chunks of melted biscuit clung to his contented cheeks.

I sent a heart emoji and put my phone away.

The bus arrived out of sync with the timetable but complete with a sullen driver and an array of passengers that could have been on any UK bus, except for the tanned skin which was the product of actual time spent in the sun and not out of a bottle.

I sat down behind a wizened lady dressed in black who bent over a shopping trolley as she adjusted her headscarf. Two teenagers shared a set of headphones and nodded along to a beat. A man talked to himself about the price of fish, but he mumbled so I may have got the translation wrong. Someone else was in the middle of an argument with someone on the phone. From the sounds of it, they weren't happy with the choice of restaurant for tonight and there was a big debate about where to go.

I settled down to read something on my phone – a research article on linguistics – and tuned everything out. So much so that I almost missed my stop and had to run out of the bus, my leather satchel slapping against my thigh.

Today was about being a typical tourist – I planned to wander the streets and maybe take in the Colosseum and the Palatine hill opposite it.

Everyone ignored me as I strolled along the pavements, taking pictures of signs and buildings as I went. I turned a corner and stopped. Part of an ancient ruin stuck out of a modern block of flats. It was surreal. As if there was too much history here, so people had to subsume it into their later structures, making a strange mix of ancient architecture and concrete. Or perhaps the city fought against the modernisation by insisting its historic foundations stayed visible.

I moved on, threading my way through the crowds that thickened as I got closer to the Colosseum. As it came into sight, it did not disappoint.

It was enormous. I waited with a group of tourists to cross the lanes of traffic that surrounded the structure. It was amazing that the locals were so used to it, they could use it as a roundabout without a second thought, but the mix of cars and Roman building was an anomaly to me.

I walked past the fake centurions charging for pictures and bought a ticket to go inside. Up close, the creamy building was dirtier than it looked from afar, stained with years of pollution.

Inside, I felt like I was in the carcass of an old animal stripped bare so that onlookers could gawp at it. I clutched my satchel closer, a shiver passing down my spine, and kept moving.

A guide passed me, speaking to a group of English tourists about the building's past. I heard him tell them that the reason it was in such disrepair was not all due to the ravages of time but more that locals had taken to looting it for cheap building materials until the government put a stop to it.

Sadness settled over me like a small dark cloud. Why couldn't people respect the past? If I had something like the Colosseum on my doorstep, I'd work to protect it, not tear it down.

Making my way across the wooden walkway, I peered into the under-floor layout of gladiator cells and animal pens, trying to imagine the building in its full glory.

What would it have been like when it was full to capacity with cheering crowds watching the latest spectacle? How could they flood it for the famous sea battles re-enacted here?

I scoured the stones for any sign of the dragon that Emperor Antonius Pius was said to have brought into the arena and thought I saw a few scorch marks blacken the off-white blocks. But it could have just been dirt.

As I gazed at the holding pens, my heart squeezed like someone had grabbed it. People and animals were kept here against their will. The arena was more oppressive than I had expected, and I left feeling sorry for all those slaves and animals forced to fight for the pleasure of the crowds.

That cloud hung over me all day as I moved on to the Palatine Hill.

Chapter 15

The Palatine Hill was more open than the Colosseum, and I wandered through the lonely pillars of abandoned temples and palaces.

This was the heart of Rome. If you believed the legends, the cave where a huge she-wolf suckled Romulus and Remus was on this hill.

It was easier here to forget the more distasteful parts of history and focus on the glory of cosmopolitan Rome, but the gnawing feeling that slaves had built most of this in its heyday worked through my bones as I ambled around.

I wondered how many supernaturals had been pressed into service and if any gnomes had been among them. My chest tightened again. Gnomes are weak – physically, I mean – and easy to subdue compared to other races like, say, trolls.

But a gnome would be better suited as an architect than a builder. I didn't think the ancient Romans cared. This whole place was built on blood, and it marred my enjoyment of the history.

I paused on some steps to eat my lunch and look out over the city of contradictions. Old and new in competition with each other and yet blending together in a strange, compelling way.

Around my neck, the dragon scale heated in its setting, absorbing the sun. I reapplied my sun cream, wiping off a smear that fell on the gold mount.

After lunch, I forced myself to walk around the entire complex and pay homage to the unsung builders that made this place possible. Some were paid – I knew that much of Roman history – but not all.

I returned to the Vegoias in a sombre mood that didn't fit with the evening Mamma Vegoia had planned.

As I walked up to the house, she popped her head out from behind a motorbike and informed me that she had prepared a proper meal to celebrate Marco's homecoming and my visit.

My heart sank. I wanted to sit alone in my room and stew, maybe share my observations with my followers and do some work on my thesis, but how could I say no to this big-hearted woman who had taken me in and shown me so much love?

So, I nodded and went inside to the sound of metal twisting as she tinkered with the engine.

I found Marco sitting outside on a sun lounger, looking like he was posing for a photo shoot. It was criminal how good he looked, while I was a dusty mess from my day in the city.

"How was the Colosseum?" he asked in Italian.

I made a face. "Not what I expected."

"It never is. But when in Rome…"

"You have to visit," I finished.

He raised his glass of iced lemonade at me. "You should stay and relax with me."

"But I might never get another chance to visit, and it's not very interesting for my channel if I laze around all day." I sank into the matching sun lounger set up under a lemon tree and poured myself a glass of homemade lemonade from the pitcher on the small mosaic table that sat between the two seats.

He shrugged and sipped his drink. "You are on holiday, why care about people you have never met?"

Giacomo chose that moment to dart down from his tree, launching himself at me. This time I caught him but didn't factor in the glass in my hand and spilled lemonade down my front.

"You are a troublesome jaculus," I said, running my hand down his bronze scales. He was smooth and warm and wriggled under my touch, pressing himself into my palm for more cuddles.

I refilled my glass, took a drink, and sighed with pleasure at the sharp but sweet taste that slipped through my mouth.

Marco regarded me with an expectant look on his face. One eyebrow quirked the tiniest fraction and his dark eyes intense as he studied me. The jaculus hadn't distracted him from his question. As I stroked the winged serpent, I considered why I cared so much about my followers.

How could I explain that these people were like family? That I had turned to the internet when my blood relations had shunned me for something I couldn't and didn't want to change about myself.

Things were better now, but when I had started my online videos and thrown myself into my passion for dragons, I was in a dark place and the people I communicated with online made me feel like I belonged to a community when I wasn't welcome in my own home.

I couldn't abandon them for a couple of weeks to enjoy myself. I owed them.

So, I snapped a picture of the lemonade and shared that. I considered including Giacomo in my post, but I didn't want to flood the Vegoias with dragon seekers hoping for a peek at the almost extinct jaculus.

Marco sighed but stayed silent. That was the best thing about my flatmate; he let me live my life. Unless my books took over the shared living space, then he had lots to say about my choices.

We sat there, two companions enjoying a break from life in Cardiff when his mother burst through the patio doors.

"Who can help with the vegetables?"

We sighed in unison and struggled up from our loungers and into the kitchen, leaving Giacomo to retreat to his tree.

Chapter 16

I awoke from my food coma to sounds of clattering plates in the kitchen. I checked the time. Too early. Again.

Groaning, I headed for the shower and then back to my room. I chose a flowing dress with a dragon print that fell below my knees and pulled my hair back from my face before heading into the kitchen.

A couple of days into my stay and there was already a routine established; the entire family gathered around the table, already halfway through breakfast, as I stumbled in and slumped into one of the wooden chairs at the table. A glass of ice-cold orange juice awaited me on the table next to some bread. I had eaten more carbs here than I did in a week at home, but when in Rome…

"What's your plan for today?"

I tensed at Giulia's question. I wanted to spend some time alone, wandering the city, but that sounded rude. As I finished my mouthful, I resigned myself to having her tag along. Giulia was great. I really liked her. But….is it wrong to want to be alone sometimes?

I swallowed and forced a bright smile. These people had welcomed me into their home. If the price was company, then I'd pay it. After all, I could be alone with the nuns. They'd chosen to live apart from the world, so weren't likely to want my company.

"I'm going back to the city. Thought I'd see some more sights."

Giulia nodded. "Have fun."

"You don't want to come?" Now I sounded desperate.

"I have things to do today, but we can spend time together this evening, if you like?"

I nodded and took another quick bite of my bread and jam. Lorenzo and Marco started bickering about some sports team, but it was too early in the morning for me to pretend to care, so I stayed quiet, finished my breakfast, and headed out into the morning sunshine.

One benefit to waking up ahead of my usual time was that the day hadn't yet had time to reach its scorching afternoon temperatures. I stretched in the cool breeze and waited for the bus.

It was late. But I didn't care. I spent the time scribbling notes for my thesis until it arrived. I wanted to maximise my study time at the abbey so any pre-work I could do now would help in the long run. Look at me, planning like a mature adult.

The driver ignored me as I paid the fare and took a seat. Somehow the bus was already sticky and too hot, so I got off a couple of stops early to walk the rest of the way.

It was freeing to abandon any plans and wander around Rome. For the first time in a long time, I had no objectives; no work deadlines, no need to be somewhere at a specific time and no need to worry about my thesis – that would be done in a matter of weeks as soon as I'd accessed the Sisters of San Silvestro's library.

So, I let my feet lead me on, choosing side streets and cutting through leafy parks as I felt like it.

A smattering of sweaty people in suits hurried past, and scooters and cars raced along dusty roads, sending clouds of smoky exhaust into the air.

Another contradiction. There was a slow pace of life here, one that enjoyed meals and talking with family and took its time, but also an undeniable need to get places fast.

I passed by the long queue to get into the Vatican on one of its scheduled open days. It was tempting to join the line, but I felt the need to keep moving and shuffling in a crowd didn't appeal to me.

Besides, they had rejected my application to research in their formidable archives because I submitted it too late for this trip. It was easy if you were a fictional symbologist on the trail of an ancient conspiracy, but if you had genuine research to do, then the process was a lot more difficult.

I sighed at all that knowledge that I couldn't access. The university computers couldn't load the vast online record, so the manuscripts and their potential were unavailable to me. But the Sisters of San Silvestro had records aplenty. A shiver of anticipation ran up my spine.

Walking away from the Vatican, I took random turns, passing small shops and a gelateria selling bright, creamy ice cream. I bought a raspberry sorbet and sent a picture to Amethyst.

She replied with a drooling face and a stream of baby pictures. A frown creased my forehead. I loved my friend, but did having a baby turn her into someone who couldn't talk about anything else?

I bit my lip as I thought up a reply when a hot prickle ran up the back of my neck.

Chapter 17

I took out my phone and held it up, posing as the perfect tourist taking a wide shot of the crowd while I scanned for the thing that made my skin crawl.

Nothing out of the ordinary.

But the hot tingle continued.

Frowning, I turned and forced myself to stroll at an unhurried pace towards a building.

I ducked into a doorway and bent over, taking my water bottle from my satchel, and surveying the street. With my other hand, I undid my bracelet and flicked my wrist, transforming it into a dagger. Thank you, Maxi – our tech support and ingenious inventor – and your experimental weapons. It was the only way I could take a blade through customs, and I had worked at the MLO long enough now that I felt naked without a weapon.

Since I joined the Magical Liaison Office, I'd taken to always carrying at least one knife. Just in case. My blades were balanced well, and I had practiced enough in the dedicated training room to know that I could hit a playing card at thirteen feet, either straight or with spin.

I palmed the blade and flicked it under the sleeve of my dress, glad I hadn't opted for short sleeves, and scanned the streets again.

I took a drink of water, considering. I had two options; stick around and try to find whatever gave me the heebie jeebies or get out of here.

Mysteries were my kryptonite. Part of the reason dragons were so fascinating to me was that we knew so little about them, even though live dragons had been back in the world for years now.

So, I knew what I would do; try to figure this out.

Keeping the bottle in one hand and my knife in the other, I slung my bag onto my shoulder and strode back out towards the Vatican, as if I'd decided to join the snaking queue. I threaded my way through the crowd, my senses on high alert.

A camera flash made me jump. I squirted my water bottle at a suspicious-looking man and received a barrage of swear words in return.

Just a tourist in a questionable outfit. Who wears a black shirt with jeans in this heat?

There were too many people.

If there was something here and it was after me, there could be casualties.

I pressed on and made it out the other side. The feeling of unease continued to swell against my neck.

If someone was after me, I should leave.

Frustrated at the lack of knowledge about the threat, but unwilling to risk innocent tourists, I hurried off, following a main street until the first turning.

I darted into the smaller side street and pressed my back against the wall, waiting.

Adrenaline prickled under my skin, and I gripped the handle of my knife tight.

But nothing more dangerous than a group of tourists and a couple of lone explorers in cargo shorts walked past.

I stayed there for another minute before stepping out of the side street. The uncomfortable feeling had disappeared. I downed what was left of my water and started walking. My fast pace matched my whirling thoughts.

The further I got from the Vatican, the more I convinced myself that it was nothing. My instincts were normally spot on, so I was confident that someone had watched me. But their motives might not have been bad. Another supernatural sensed me, perhaps, wondering if a small gnome was a threat to them.

Or maybe I'd wandered into a warded territory. It made sense that the Vatican would have magical workings around it to protect and preserve their treasures.

I was paranoid. Too much time in the Magical Liaison Office made me think the worst of everyone. Not surprising when we dealt with the dregs of the supernatural world; those who tried to destroy the delicate balance between magical beings and mundanes, either through malice or stupidity.

Shaking my head, I took in my surroundings. I had crossed the river at some point and was in a large piazza. Trendy bars and restaurants lined the square, and a phallic Egyptian style obelisk marked the centre while statues of gods reclined on stone waves above a fountain at its base.

Behind the towering stone needle, a domed building in pale bricks dominated the square.

I checked my location on my phone; Piazza Navona next to the Fountain of the Four Rivers. Made sense.

Zooming out, I could see the Trevi Fountain, and the Pantheon were close by. On impulse, I decided to grab a salad and head for the famous fountain first.

After eating in the shade, I took a longer route to the Trevi Fountain, but hadn't made it past the first side street when I saw a sign for a library.

I hesitated for a moment, but I was here for myself. This was my holiday and if I wanted to spend it in a library, I could. Excited by the prospect, I didn't even post it online. This would be my secret escape.

I wandered in, my canvas shoes slapping on the tiled floor, and breathed a sigh of relief at the cooler indoor temperature. My sigh turned into a gasp as I took in the wondrous interior.

It was like something out of a film. Wooden shelves held tightly packed leather-bound books that stretched up three stories until they finished just below the bright, domed roof.

On each floor, there was a balcony and ladders to allow readers access to the higher shelves.

Book display stands held curated texts open on interesting pages. I bounced on my feet. This was my definition of perfection.

A quiet librarian asked if they could help in the hushed tones of someone who shared my reverence for knowledge. I asked for the catalogue, and they directed me to a computer site, the only concession to modern technology.

I quickly gave up on the catalogue and let instinct guide me, walking up the spiral marble staircase to the higher levels as carved reliefs of earlier patrons stared down at me.

I smiled up at them. I bet they'd never thought a purple-haired lesbian gnome would grace these halls when they'd built it.

I whiled away the rest of the day choosing books and skimming through them, settling down to read if something took my fancy. Perfect.

Chapter 18

That evening, Giulia took me to a local bar at the insistence of Mamma Vegoia. The older woman still tried to push us together, and honestly, after my day in the library, I was open to the magia dell'Italia.

Giulia ordered us two glasses of chianti that came from some Etruscan vineyards, and I sipped the rich red wine with pleasure.

"Are you learning to appreciate the now?" Giulia asked, peering at me over her large glass.

"I'm getting there," I said.

A man eyed us over Giulia's shoulder. I groaned. I knew what was coming. He didn't disappoint. Moments later, the moustachioed would-be Lothario swaggered over and pulled up a chair. "Ciao bellas, are you looking for a good time?"

I rolled my eyes. Some types of men were the same in any country; the type who couldn't believe that two women out for a drink wouldn't be interested in them.

"No," I said.

Giulia snorted into her glass. It felt good to make someone laugh, and Giulia's chortle was a thing of beauty, like a splashing fountain on a summer's day. But it wasn't the ethereal magic of Shesalva's elven giggle that warmed my soul. If Giulia was a fountain, then Shesalva was the rain, grounding me, nourishing me. I felt a stab of something like guilt twist through me. Nope. She left me. I had to remind myself of that. I didn't owe her anything. I pushed away thoughts of my ex, turning guilt into anger as I concentrated on the dzraker still hitting on Giulia.

"Don't worry." The man waggled his eyebrows. "I've got more than enough for both of you." He placed a hand on Giulia's leg.

"Not interested," she said before sending a stream of Italian curses his way. This woman swore so hard it would make an Italian sailor blush, and I loved it.

"Maybe you haven't met the right man yet, bella." Classic chat up line. Even in Italian, it sounded cheesy with the undertone of menace that suggested he couldn't believe he wasn't everyone's dream boy.

I had my bracelet off my wrist and into my hand in its knife form in less than a second, but Giulia covered his hand with hers and said, "You will leave us alone or my mother will curse your family, and you can tell your nonna that it is your fault that your testicles have shrivelled into useless sacks and she will never get grandbabies."

"Grandbabies? We need to get a lot closer to think about children, bella." He wormed his way closer and ran a finger down her arm.

"Leave us alone." I didn't bother with threats of curses; the prick of my knife on his skin sent its own message.

He swallowed before the anger flared in his eyes. "Stupid puttana, and I don't even know who your mother is." The man spat on the floor at our feet.

Giulia's smile put me in mind of a snake about to strike. "Mamma Vegoia."

The man shrank back, pulling his hand away from Giulia like she'd stuck a pin in him He stared at the gobbet of saliva on the bar floor as if he could take it back before scurrying over to his corner of the bar where he huddled over his lager while shooting us nervous looks every few seconds.

"That's some threat," I said, putting my bracelet back on.

Giulia nodded, and her posture relaxed as she sipped her wine. "Everyone round here knows mamma. And no one wants to upset her."

Chapter 19

And so, the rest of my fortnight with the Vegoias passed. I divided my time between visiting traditional sites in the morning and then retreating to the welcoming cool of the fascinating library before returning home to indulge in Mamma Vegoia's cooking and cuddles with the jaculus.

The prickling sensation of someone watching me returned at the Pantheon, but I couldn't pinpoint the source. It was a speck of unease that marred my trip, like a burr stuck in my shoe; annoying, but not enough to ruin the joy.

By the time it got to the last night, I felt truly relaxed for the first time in a long time. I had spent two weeks doing what I wanted, discovering the past and reading new books in a beautiful library. Bliss.

A wave of sadness washed over me as I brushed down my clean jeans – I could barely do them up thanks to a fortnight of great food – and headed outside for the last family meal I would have with the Vegoias.

I was early, for once, and wandered the lush grove of the garden. Giacomo leapt down to my shoulders, knocking me off balance, and I stumbled through a curtain of hanging vines.

I opened my mouth, ready to scold the winged serpent when the cobweb sensation of magic prickled over my skin, making the hairs rise along my arms.

Giulia and Mamma Vegoia held hands over the small fountain. A soft yellow light grew around them before dissipating in tiny sparks of starlight around the garden.

"What the dzrak?" The words fell out of my mouth in English before I could stop them.

They were magic users. And I'd had no idea.

"Aloora!" Was that surprise or guilt on Giulia's face?

Mamma wasn't embarrassed at all. "You have arrived just in time to see our evening blessing."

I twisted one foot on the large paving slab just outside the vines. "Should I go?"

"There is no need. The magic is done. And, come here," Mamma Vegoia beckoned me over and I joined them next to the gurgling fountain, intrigued and wary. "We will give you a blessing for your journey."

They joined hands around me, and I felt self-conscious as Giulia smiled down at me. Both women closed their eyes and led a chant. I picked out the odd word – blessing, fortune – before a warm, loving sensation swelled over me.

The chanting stopped, but the comforting feeling stayed.

"Now you will have a good onward journey."

"Thank you, but what…?" I trailed off. It was rude to ask what someone's species was.

Mamma Vegoia smiled. "We are descendants of an Etruscan nymph, here long before the Romans claimed this land. This is our grove." She gestured to the well cared for garden. "We work small magics and try to make the world a better place, but it is hard. Despite the dragons now alive, there is so much pollution now that our power is smaller than our ancestors."

Giacomo gave a hiss as if he agreed with Mamma Vegoia's words.

"But we have high hopes for renewable energy," Giulia added, "and Mamma is working on alternative fuels."

I nodded, in a daze. It was a lot to take in. But the alternative fuels explained why a nature-loving nymph would have a motorcycle. Something Mamma said tugged at my brain.

"Why did you say, 'despite the dragons'?"

She looked at me. "The link between dragons and magic is well known, when they died out – or hibernated, as it seems – magic weakened. Now they are back, it is stronger. We can feel it in our spells. I thought you studied dragons?"

"Mamma!" Giulia admonished.

"It's OK. I hadn't thought of that link." Mentally, I kicked myself. Magic was stronger with dragons in the world. I hadn't noticed because my magic, such as it was, was latent and not noticeable to begin with. I could sense things sometimes, but I couldn't cast spells or use runes to make enchantments. This was a fascinating route to study…but my elven academic liaison, Professor Maron, might have a heart attack if I asked to change my thesis topic again.

I became aware that both Vegoias were staring at me as I thought.

"And Marco?" He'd never once used magic in our shared apartment. I was sure of that.

Mamma shook her head. "Our magic passes down through the females of the family. My boys are normal, if a little luckier, perhaps, than most mundanes."

"Cool," I said, unsure what else to say. Giacomo pressed his chin into my palm, nudging for cuddles. I rewarded him by tickling under his chin. "So, what now?"

"Now, we eat." Mamma Vegoia swept into the kitchen, leaving me standing outside with Giulia, who shrugged.

"I didn't mean about food…" I said.

"I know. You meant about the spell." Giulia understood me. "It's not permanent, but it will give you good fortune."

"I'll need it." Now that the holiday part of my stay was coming to an end, the monster of my thesis loomed large ahead of me.

My problem was that I wasn't a planner. I preferred to go off on tangents, discover new research and cram the writing in as close to the deadline as possible. A technique that worked well for a couple of thousand-word essays, but which had let me down for my sixty-thousand-word PhD thesis. I had a month to write something the equivalent of a novel and even the ever-patient Professor Maron had told me there were no more extensions to the deadline. This was it.

But maybe the spell worked, because somehow, I felt like I could do it, despite the paltry number of words I had written down to date.

Chapter 20

I didn't have time to dwell on my thesis – or lack of – because Mamma Vegoia called from the kitchen for help in a colourful way with language that made me see where Giulia got her vocabulary from, and we all convened in the stuffy room, made hot from the oven, to chop, slice and carry as needed.

Soon enough, we were outside seated at a table overladen with salads and pasta. Giacomo snuck under the table, waiting for scraps that might fall. I felt his smooth tail around my ankle – I guess he'd adopted me.

Mamma Vegoia served us all generous portions, and I ate with gusto, savouring the simple homemade pasta in a tangy pesto sauce and the fresh tomato and mozzarella salad sprinkled with basil leaves. Perfection.

No sooner had we finished than Mamma dashed into the kitchen and came back bearing an entire stuffed salmon, its head and tail poking over the end of the enormous serving dish.

My eyes popped. The pasta was just a starter, and I was already full. Rookie mistake.

I asked for a small portion, but Mamma Vegoia laughed and cut me a thick slice of the salmon. At least it was vaguely healthy…

As I tucked in, Lorenzo topped off my wine glass and I decided to give in and treat this feast like Christmas, accepting that I would overeat and tomorrow it would be back to normal. The nuns' diet had to be healthier anyway. Whoever heard of an unhealthy nun?

But when Mamma brought out the lasagne, I almost spat the honey-coloured wine out over the table. She couldn't expect us to eat that as well, surely? I insisted on the smallest square of the cheesy meaty deliciousness and toyed with it on my plate. No wonder Italian meals took so long when there were this many courses.

Everyone else slowed down as well, taking their time over their food.

"So, Aloora, what has been your favourite part of Rome?" Giulia asked, her eyes sparkling.

"The library." I smiled at the memory of its laden shelves and papery treasures.

She laughed, and the others chuckled along.

"You come all the way to Italy for books when you already have too many at home." Marco shook his head, but he tempered his comment with a smile, so I knew he was joking.

"The sights are nice too. I think Herculaneum was my favourite."

"And the food. You liked the pizza place, yes?" Lorenzo asked, leaning forward.

"The pizza was to die for," I agreed.

He leaned back and sighed. "It is," he whispered, transported back to his own fond memories of the place.

"The pineapple was particularly tasty."

Lorenzo spat out the mouthful of wine he'd just sipped. I raised my glass to him with a smile and the family roared with laughter while Lorenzo cursed the inventor of the Hawaiian pizza. Giulia gave my knee a conspiratorial squeeze.

When the chuckles died down, I coughed, "I wanted to thank you all. You've been the family I always wanted, and it means so much that you've welcomed me into your home when you didn't have to. Grazie mille, for your acceptance, for your amazing food, Mamma, and for everything." I lifted my glass in a toast.

The Vegoias raised their own wine glasses and toasted back.

Mamma had a broad smile on her face and a tear in her brown eyes as she said, "It was nothing. You are welcome anytime, especially when you are such an easy house guest. Now, come, the dessert is ready."

As Marco and Lorenzo dished up the creamy tiramisu, I unbuttoned the top button of my jeans to allow my growing stomach some space. This was the most food I'd ever eaten in one sitting.

The evening drifted into night and bats swooped overhead, catching the tiny insects that buzzed about the garden, we finished our meal.

Everyone helped clear the table, and when that was done, I took my glass outside. I wanted to bottle this evening of familial bliss forever and I wasn't quite ready for it to end.

Chapter 21

I sat on the edge of the small fountain and allowed my fingers to trail in the cold, clear water. Giacomo joined me, sticking his snout into the water before sneezing.

Giulia stroked his back as she sat next to me and poured some more wine into my glass.

"This is a special wine made by family in Siena. They say it is touched by magic."

I raised an eyebrow at her. "Is it?"

"Well, perhaps there is a little of the magia dell'Italia in the region. They are a lot closer to nature than we are in the city and Vegoia's original spring is in Chiusi, so many of our relatives live near there."

"Why do you stay here?"

She sighed and dipped her own fingers in the water. "This is our home. Etruscans were here long before even the Romans, and we have love for the region and hope that our presence tempers some of the destruction and pollution in the city. Besides, it's not so bad here."

Her voice turned husky, and I looked away and sipped my wine. It was delicious, like honeyed fruits cascading in my mouth.

"I have something for you." Giulia pulled a ring from her finger. She laughed at my awkward expression. "It is not a proposal. It is a gift."

She pushed it onto my little finger, and I admired the band. A bright blue charm in the shape of an eye stared back at me.

"It is for protection and luck. It will ward off evil."

"Thank you." I rummaged in my bag and pulled out a piece of paper. I wasn't a gifted artist, but I'd copied the picture of Giulia and me at Herculaneum onto paper.

"Grazie." She accepted it like it was a priceless Picasso and trailed one finger down the picture. "That was a good day."

I smiled. "It was."

Her dark eyes assessed me, and she pushed a strand of my violet hair away from my face. Giulia leaned into me. I froze. She caught my awkwardness and paused.

The jaculus broke the tension by diving into the fountain and splashing us both.

I stammered an apology. Giulia was lovely – dark, interesting – just the sort of girl I should like, but…I didn't. Not in that way. And I'd given out the wrong sort of signals. Again. Story of my dzraking life. Now I ruined friendships as well as relationships, it seemed.

"It is alright, Aloora." My name sounded like a purr on her lips. "You are heart sick."

"I…" I had no idea what to say.

"You pine for another. It is alright. We are friends. I will not force myself on you. I thought we might have…but your heart is somewhere else, back in Wales."

I hung my head. "Is it that obvious?"

Giulia laughed. "Yes. I thought you might have got over her with a little help from la magia dell'Italia. But you are not yet ready to move on."

I looked deep into the fountain that sparkled as it reflected the lights shining from the house, and I admitted the truth out loud. "Not yet, but I'm moving forward."

"Yes," Giulia beamed, "and if you change your mind about living with nuns, you can come find me in Rome."

I snorted out a laugh and for the first time in a long time, I truly felt like myself. It was the perfect end to the first leg of my journey.

Chapter 22

The next morning was another early start. The smell of sweet pastries and bitter coffee greeted me, and I wandered into the kitchen where Marco's family waited.

I knew they would want a big goodbye, but I had overindulged in wine last night and my head pounded. I wore dark sunglasses and the loosest dress I had packed, not trusting that I could still fit into anything more form fitting after the amount of carbs and sugar I had eaten in the past two weeks.

Mamma pressed a glass of juice into my hand and a pastry into my bag 'for the journey'.

"Remember, come find me if you need to escape the nuns," Giulia whispered in my ear.

I smiled and nodded, not trusting myself to reply through the lump in my throat. Instead, I moved on to Marco, who hugged me and said he would see me back in Cardiff.

"Don't fill the flat with more furniture while I'm not there."
I tried to sound stern, but he just grinned back at me like I had
issued a challenge.

I should have been more worried, but any anxiety was lost
in the overpowering sadness at leaving the Vegoias and the
rush of excitement that came from knowing I was heading into
unchartered research. And I got to drive there.

My fingers itched as I flung the suitcase into the boot of
Lorenzo's Fiat 500. He had offered to loan me the car, but I
wanted more from Italy than a battered Fiat, so instead, he
promised to drive me to a car hire place where I had reserved
the fastest car I could afford on my MLO salary. The rental
place had been surprisingly affordable, so I was expecting it
to be dented, but I didn't care. I wanted horsepower so I could
gallop along the Italian motorway.

We drove in companionable silence to the rental shop. By
which I mean that I closed my eyes while the sound of euro
pop played on the dodgy radio and Lorenzo cursed at any car
or pedestrian within five feet. My lips curved upwards. I
would miss the Vegoia siblings.

We arrived at the car hire place in record time and Lorenzo
screeched to a halt.

"Do you want me to stay?" he asked with one eye on a police
officer resting on his bike and drinking a coffee at the café
across the street.

"No, thanks." I grabbed my bag from the boot and slammed
it shut, now used to the car's quirks. "Thanks for everything,
Lorenzo. I hope the job hunting goes well."

He blinked at me in surprise. "I have a job. Mamma just doesn't think that an app consultant is proper work." Lorenzo shrugged like it was a cross he bore.

"Wow, that's…wow." I stared at him. Looks like the whole Vegoia family was full of surprises.

Across the street, the officer finished his coffee. Lorenzo revved his engine.

"It's a shame you're in love with someone else. You and Giulia would make a cute couple."

"I'm not–"

He sped off into the morning traffic.

"–in love with someone else," I said to the street. Well, I hadn't thought of a certain red-headed elf for at least twenty-four hours, so I was on the road to recovery.

And I had a month at an abbey focusing on my first love; dragons. If that wasn't a remedy for a broken heart, I didn't know what was.

But first, the rental car.

I dragged my bag through the glazed doors and to the desk where a pencil-thin attendant tapped at a computer screen. I coughed to get her attention, and she held up one long finger topped with an inch-long crimson nail while she clacked at the keyboard with her other hand.

The office was bare with faded walls that were a shade of non-descript grey I didn't think you could find outside of UK government offices, but apparently Italian rental places had the same paint supplier.

I kicked the tall desk with my boots while I waited. The lady gave me a severe look. It paired well with her hair, which was pulled back into the tightest bun I had ever seen. I almost saluted her.

I picked up the pen, connected to the desk by a silver chain to prevent biro thieves from taking it, scrawled on the pad of paper in front of me, and held it up to her.

With a drawn-out sigh, she stopped typing and raised one pencilled on eyebrow while pursing her red lips. She aimed for annoyed but ended up looking constipated.

I gave her a bright smile and spoke in fluent Italian. "I'm here for a car."

"Everybody who comes here wants a car." She remained unimpressed.

"Yes, but I have one reserved." My fingers twitched. I couldn't wait to get my hands on the sporty number I had picked out.

"Name?"

"Aloora Dragonquest." I spelled out my chosen surname. Italian didn't have much call for 'q's, and why would it? The language was sinfully romantic with its long vowels and playful double 'z's. It scorned the harder letters, and rightly so.

She asked for my driver's license and there was a long wait while she reconciled my birth name with my chosen one. Not for the first time, I wondered why I didn't just change it legally. Neebly was a crap name. So unassuming and gnomish.

But something in me wanted to keep a connection with my family, even if they didn't want to keep one with me.

I tried to explain this to the uncaring assistant, but she was only interested in getting the name on her system to match with my ID.

"Automatic or manual?"

I walked my fingers along the desk and tried for flirty. "I can handle anything."

She stared at me.

"I reserved a manual."

"Yes, I see. But the car is not in stock at this branch."

"So, you're upgrading me to a Ferrari?" I could hope.

The assistant almost laughed. I swear her lips twitched. "No, it is still the same make."

Good, a nice sporty number, just what I wanted. She had me sign a triplicate form and asked me if I wanted the extra insurance. I went for it, just to see if it would get her to smile.

Nothing.

Maybe she wasn't on commission.

She handed over some keys and made me sign something else before asking if I needed help getting it out of the parking space.

I laughed and pocketed the keys. "No, thanks."

Dragging my suitcase, I followed the direction of her blood-red nails to the row of parking spaces out front. There was a sleek convertible waiting for me in the middle. I quickened my pace, imagining how responsive it would be.

I clicked the keys and heard the lock depress. But when I went to open the boot, nothing happened. I tried again. Same result.

On the third go, I realised that the car next to it had unlocked. A piece of schiztz or, in Italian, *pezzo di merda* car that looked like it wouldn't make it out of the carpark, let alone to the abbey.

Chapter 23

I left my luggage in the car park and stormed back in.

"There's been a mistake."

"No mistake."

"I wanted a sporty little convertible. How am I meant to enjoy the open road in that?"

"All convertibles are taken."

"What about the one right there in the car park?"

"Reserved."

"By me!"

"I am sorry, there is no mistake. You wanted an Alfa Romeo, you got one."

"It's tiny."

"Compact."

I tried to wheedle her into giving me another car, but she wouldn't budge. That flash of amusement I'd tried so hard to get out of her was now growing by the minute as she refused to give me anything better than the piece of crap she'd already assigned me.

In the end, I gave up and went to get my car. So much for the Vegoia's blessing to have a good onward journey. My suitcase barely fit in the tiny boot, and I slammed it shut in anger before climbing into the front seat and posting my dismay online.

After a brief fight with the gear stick, the car finally agreed that I was in charge, and I was off, following the electronic commands of my phone's sat nav as it directed me out of the city.

Manoeuvring around the streets of Rome was part terrifying, part exhilarating and my anger dissipated as I sank into the flow of driving. I soon found the Roman rhythm of accelerating, harsh braking, and cursing at anyone else on the road.

It was so much better than driving at home, where there were more constrained expectations of motorists. Here I could change lanes at will with a blast of my horn. It was like street racing at low speeds.

And then I made it out of the city and headed onto the motorway towards the abbey. The tension eased from my shoulders as the car responded to my foot on the pedal and the traffic eased off. I rolled down the window and rested my arm on the door, tapping along to the beat of some Italian rap playing on the radio. They didn't seem to have any of the fantasy metal I preferred and there wasn't a Bluetooth hookup for my phone, but the music was upbeat, and I pressed down on the accelerator, zooming along the main road as fast as the crappy car would go.

There weren't many other cars, but the road wasn't clear either, so when the black sedan first pulled into view, I thought nothing of it.

It stayed two car lengths behind me for half an hour, not moving to overtake anything until I pulled out to pass a slower moving red van. Weird. The black car could race past my crappy, ancient Alfa Romeo if it chose, so why would it hang back?

Nothing about driving in Italy so far convinced me that a motorist would keep their distance out of a desire for safety or respect for others on the road.

Of course, perhaps they were a tourist, scared of keeping up with the Italian driving style.

I experimented by slamming the accelerator to the floor. The sedan sped up, matching my speed.

That prickle of unease I'd felt in Rome crept back along my spine. Someone was following me.

Chapter 24

The obvious question was: 'Why would anyone be following me?'

But I couldn't get an answer to that without stopping to ask, and the type of people who tail others in black sedans are the sort who tend to ask the questions, not answer them.

I went through the options in my head. I could pull over and see what happened. One hand drifted from the steering wheel to my knife bracelet. Tempting. But I didn't want to get deported before I'd finished my research.

Option two, then, was to lose them. There were some problems with that option. I chewed my lip as I worked through the issues; first, I was on a main road with nowhere to go except straight on and, second, I was in a crappy car that wouldn't beat a snail in a car chase, let alone the sleek beast following me.

The one thing in my favour was that my vehicle wasn't exactly memorable, so maybe it was a good thing I hadn't got the sporty number I'd wanted.

"OK, Scrappy," I said, naming the car, "let's see if this dzraker is following us for sure."

I pulled off the motorway. The sedan followed. When I found a suitable junction, I took the next turning sharply without indicating, and headed into a picturesque town filled with cobbled streets and houses that butted up against one another. But my pursuer was prepared for this classic move and followed, also without indicating. It could be a coincidence that the sedan turned off here, but I didn't think so. I didn't believe in coincidences, and I wasn't about to start now.

But I did believe in technology. So, I wedged my phone onto the dashboard and zoomed out as far as I could on the sat nav map.

I cracked my knuckles and accelerated sharply, weaving in and out of the cars ahead of me as I darted through the narrow streets in this small town.

Buildings flashed past, too fast for me to get anything other than a tantalising taste of their architecture as I sped on, screeching round corners.

The sat nav shouted at me to take the next left, but I wanted to lose whoever was behind me before I got back onto the main road, so I swung right down a tiny, cobbled street.

A trio of elderly women dressed in black cursed as I passed, wheels screeching. They shook their fists at me as I skidded past a group of men playing cards, causing a slipstream that pulled their deck off the table and trailed cards behind me like I was some sort of crazed magician.

I risked a glance in my rear-view mirror and saw the sedan turning still on my tail and gaining.

I needed a new plan. My fingers itched as my palms grew sweaty. I drove on, my body acting on autopilot as I searched for a solution. The ring Giulia had given me stayed cool against my skin, helping to calm my jittery nerves. A crazy idea danced across my brain.

"So crazy, it just might work," I muttered as I swung round another corner.

I kept ahead of the car, ducking in and out of traffic, taking turns at random until I found what I wanted – a tight parking space on the street in the middle of a row of other dusty cars.

With a check of my mirrors to confirm the sedan hadn't turned after me yet, I pulled a handbrake J turn and screeched into the spot.

It was a manoeuvre I had practised at the Magical Liaison Office advanced driving course and my heart hammered in my chest, filling my ears with the sound of blood pumping as I trusted the compact car to fit in the space.

Scrappy didn't disappoint and skidded to a halt in the centre of the tiny space with the slightest of bumps to the car in front; better than much of the parking I'd seen in Rome.

I switched off the engine and ducked down, hiding my bright hair under a rag I found in the foot well. This was my one shot. They had to believe the car was empty and had been parked here all day. If not…I flicked my wrist to transform the steel bracelet into a blade and gripped my knife with my other hand…driving wasn't the only thing I'd learned working for the MLO.

The sedan sped past, not even bothering to check the parked cars as it searched for me.

"Thank you," I whispered to the ring. Don't judge me; my best friend makes magical jewellery, so it might well have been the lucky ring that saved me. I'd take any help I could get.

Intent on hiding, I didn't get a look at who was in the car or the registration plate. If I were on a job, Agent Jones would chew me out for that oversight.

As this was my personal time, safety was my number one priority and fear quelled any curiosity I had about my pursuer. For now, I just wanted to escape.

I exhaled, telling my body to calm down. I needed to think. I gave it a minute, then sat up, pulling the oily rag off my head. As I reached for the ignition, I noticed one of the elderly women pulling on the sleeve of a police officer and pointing at my car.

I groaned. You know your driving is bad when an Italian nonna complains about it.

The officer walked over, too afraid of the old woman to disobey, and knocked on my window.

Another set of choices lay before me. I could explain my situation in Italian and ask for his help as a representative of the law here – that might lead to inter-country co-operation and a lengthy sojourn at the local carabinieri while they took statements and sorted it all out – or I could play the dumb tourist.

His first words decided me. "Hello, bella, why is a gorgeous lady like you trying to get my attention with bad driving? You could have asked me out."

It was the second unwelcome male attention I'd received since arriving in the country and it made me sure he wouldn't help me in any meaningful way.

"Scusa," I replied in an exaggerated English accent, "no parlo Italiano."

His sigh was so heavy, his entire body deflated. I could see the thoughts flick through his head, playing out on his expressive face; arresting a foreign national was complicated, more than he was paid to deal with, so he gave me a lecture in Italian about my driving.

I smiled and nodded, playing dumb. Then I gave him two thumbs up and told him that the footballer Giuseppe was molto bueno in an accent that made me wince.

I asked him for help to get out of the space with lots of hand gestures and much shameless fluttering of eyelashes – I almost made myself sick with disgust – but the man actually got into the car and shunted the others out of the way for me, using a more traditional Italian approach to parking than I'd used to get into the spot.

With a wave, I drove off, more cautious this time. As soon as I turned the corner, I draped the rag over my hair again, so I didn't stand out as much in case the sedan was watching, and headed onto the nunnery.

Chapter 25

A few hours later, after taking the back roads as much as I could to avoid another run in with the black sedan, I arrived at the abbey.

It was a squat, unassuming building made of that same burnt sienna stone that was a hallmark of the Italian countryside around here. There was an archway carved into the wall and a faded sign telling me I was in the right place.

I drove through the arch, Scrappy's suspension protesting yet more uneven cobblestones, and I parked next to an ancient white car and two vespa style scooters.

For the second time today, I was glad about the car rental mix up. An ostentatious sports car would have made me even more awkward in the presence of such asceticism.

I messaged Amethyst, Marco and Giulia that I had arrived, but left out the car chase, and I got yet another picture of Dafydd, his chubby arm waving at me as his stomach burst out of a baby grow that was too small.

I looked down at my belly. After two weeks of living on fabulous Italian food, I knew that feeling.

Marco and Giulia replied telling me to be safe. I rubbed a finger over the ring that Giulia had given me. They didn't know how timely their words were.

I sent an update to my followers to let them know I was excited about this research phase of my trip – again leaving out the car chase, which now felt more like a surreal waking dream than a threat – and received a slew of support.

Dr4gonista: Sounds fun!!!

BigDragonEnergy: Saw you left Rome, sorry not to catch up with u. Where are u now?

Willowitch: Wish I was there.

The weight of my followers and the crushing need to be on all the time, always seeking the next thing to post, crashed over me like a wave. It was so much pressure, even though I loved educating people about dragons and correcting misconceptions, even thought my followers were all lovely people with a shared interest who had saved me when my family had shut me out, it was still too much. I couldn't bring myself to reply in case some of my feelings spilled onto the keyboard.

It was tempting to shut it all off and totally immerse myself in my research, live more in the moment, as Giulia had suggested. I pocketed my phone without replying.

It was like a weight lifted off me. I didn't have to respond. I took a cleansing breath, plastered a smile on my face and got out of the car.

As I headed for the tiny wooden door next to a discreet sign for the nunnery, my smile became genuine as the quiet peace of the site settled into me. This was a place of power and tranquillity. I could use some of that right now. I hoped it would help me focus on my research.

Unsure what the protocol was for entering a holy site, I hesitated before I knocked.

There was no reply, so I knocked again and waited. After the third try, I gave up on waiting and went inside. The circular handle turned with a squeak, and I squinted into the dark interior – the nuns hadn't splashed out on anything so luxurious as electricity inside their entrance hall.

I pulled my suitcase in and used the torch on my phone to make sure I didn't trip over any of the decorative tiles on the floor.

I checked the time. I was a little later than I'd said, but the nuns knew I was coming. A slight frown crinkled my brow, and I checked my emails.

Yep. There were the messages confirming my stay and date of arrival. But no one was here to meet me.

"Hello?" I called out into the empty room before repeating the call in Italian and Latin, just in case these were old school nuns.

A shuffling sound along the corridor made me squint again and my hand went to my knife, back in its bracelet form on my wrist.

"Hello?" I tried again, shining my torch towards the swishing sound.

"Aieee!" A minute nun appeared, holding her hands in front of her eyes. "Put that down, you'll blind me," she said in rapid Italian.

Muttering an apology, I lowered the light.

The nun recovered and smoothed down her habit, which was plain apart from a gold badge in the shape of a cross sewn onto the left side. There was a design in the middle of a man with a halo around his head – some sort of saint by the pious, smug look on his ancient face.

"Welcome to the Abbey of Saint Silvestro. Who are you?"

Chapter 26

Any pride I had in my research, my job, in myself as a person flooded out of me at that moment. I had travelled across Europe to study with these nuns and she had no idea who I was.

"I'm Aloora."

Polite, blank look.

"Aloora Dragonquest."

That hint of a smile didn't move.

"I emailed about studying here."

Her pale eyes held a hint of disbelief. "We do not get many visitors."

So why didn't she know who I was and why I was here? Had I come here for nothing? What would I do – what could I do – if they didn't grant me access to their library?

I tried one last time. "I wanted to study Draconic. I requested access to your archives."

"Oh! Yes, of course."

The relief that surged through me was a palpable wave that made my body sag as the tension left me.

"My apologies, but we did not think that you would come."

"Why not?" I blurted the words out, hurt that this nun wouldn't believe I would cross borders for the knowledge in their books. I would walk into a dragon's mouth for the chance to find out more about the fascinating creatures. Literally. I'd once asked Fulgor to let me see his sparker, the part of his throat that created the lightning he breathed. He'd refused. But I was willing to stick my head into his mouth to find out.

The nun gave a half shrug. "Few people come to our town to seek knowledge. They would rather visit the more touristy areas or the Vatican library."

I kept my mouth shut. The Vatican had turned me down. If they'd said yes, I might have stayed in Rome.

"But you are here." The nun smiled. "I am Sister Theresa, and I will show you to your room. But first…"

She held out her hand, palm facing up.

I stared at it. Then shook it.

She laughed, a wheezing, gulping laugh that rocked her entire body and had me moving forward to check she wasn't having a seizure.

Sister Theresa waved me away. "No. Your phone."

My fingers gripped my smartphone like it was a lifeline.

"Some of our guests like to be without technology," she said, a grin playing on her lips. "But it is your choice. It is always your choice."

Despite thinking I could turn it all off when I arrived, the reality of giving up my phone wrenched something deep inside me. That was how I knew I had to do it. Maybe this would be a good thing, some personal growth.

"How do you contact the outside world?" I stalled as I typed out frantic messages to Amethyst so at least someone would know why I was offline.

That laugh again. I worried that she might keel over from lack of oxygen, as she didn't appear to breathe in for a series of hiccupping bursts. "We are nuns. We do not seek contact with the outside world."

"What about emergencies?"

Sister Theresa blinked at me. "Our Mother Superior has a phone in her office – a landline."

I pressed send, set my status to out of office or away on every app I could think of, swallowed hard and slowly pressed my phone into her palm.

Chapter 27

It was like losing a limb. My lifeline. My communication with the outside world. I hadn't even had time to message my followers. Would they stick around without daily updates?

But I'd made my choice. It was the price I had to pay to study here, and I had to get my thesis done. I squared my shoulders, my thirst for knowledge outweighing my desire for outside connection. This would be worth it.

"Grazie. I will keep it safe."

I nodded, not trusting myself to speak around the dragon-sized lump in my throat. How could losing my phone affect me so deeply?

"Now, come, I will show you your room."

She led me down a corridor, then another. My suitcase rattled on the tiles, and I cringed with embarrassment. This place was so peaceful, and I disturbed it just by being here.

A wimpled face peeked out from a doorway as I passed, curiosity blazing over her face before she ducked back inside.

Another nun glared at me as I walked, barely concealed hatred oozing from her stare.

"Who's that?" I whispered once I was out of earshot.

"Oh, don't worry about Sister Ursula. She's stern, but we couldn't do without her."

I made a mental note to avoid Sister Ursula. She looked as if she could eat me up and spit me out before breakfast, and not in a good way.

Sister Theresa stopped in a small corridor that had three doors leading off it. "We don't get many visitors, but here are our guest rooms. There's a bathroom at the end of the hall and you can eat your meals with us."

She opened one of the small wooden doors revealing a plain room with a single bed, thin wardrobe, a tiny table, and a chair. It was a place to lie down and sleep and not much else.

Marco would love the distressed wooden furniture, although the effect was more due to age than a design choice. My hand went to my pocket to snap a quick picture for him before I remembered that Sister Theresa had my phone.

I swallowed. I had to ask. I couldn't be dishonest with nuns. "Erm, I have a laptop."

Sister Theresa looked at me with that same bland expression she'd had when I'd first arrived, like she was trying to figure me out.

"Yes?" she asked after a long pause.

"It's technology." Should I give that up too? But then how could I work?

She chewed on this for a while. "Yes?"

"My laptop. I could email people." I didn't know why I pressed the point. If I didn't use my laptop while I studied then writing everything would take twice as long, but I felt like I needed her permission.

She laughed again, her shoulders shaking as she gasped. "You cannot use email if that is your concern. We have no Wi-Fi except in Mother Superior's office. Of course, you can use your laptop to help with your research. That is why you're here, isn't it? Are you still happy with your choice to give me your phone?"

I nodded weakly, not trusting myself to speak in case my resolve weakened. I could be disconnected for a few weeks. It wouldn't kill me or hurt my followers if they didn't hear from me for a while.

"Then I will leave you to settle in and you can start tomorrow. Dinner is at six." Sister Theresa left me there, staring after her.

No Wi-Fi. It was like my world had tipped upside down.

Chapter 28

I unpacked my suitcase and stuffed it under the bed. That killed fifteen minutes. I tried out the chair – wobbly – and the desk – also wobbly – and set up my laptop.

Sister Theresa was right. No Wi-Fi. Not even a sketchy signal from someone else's network.

My first instinct was to post about the ridiculousness of the situation. But then I remembered that the nun had my phone.

The bare walls of my cell looked ominous rather than calming. The single painting of a saint stared down at me with a smug grin on his painted face.

As if he knew what I wanted and what I couldn't have.

It was fine. I could go without a phone and social media while I was here. My followers weren't flighty, they would stick by me, and even if they didn't, I had built my channel up once. I could do it again.

The urge to post came over me again in a wave.

This was a nightmare.

What I needed was something to take my mind off my disconnection.

As if in answer to my deepest thoughts, a sweet singing floated through my room. It soared through my soul, lifting me up, though I couldn't hear the words.

I had to find the source.

I left my room and padded down the corridor, following the beautiful music.

The song led me to a building I guessed was the chapel based on its stained-glass windows and large door. I paused on the threshold and let the music wash over me.

It was perfect, and the notes swirled through me, telling me of peace and joy even though I still couldn't make out the words.

I opened the door and stepped into the cool chapel, seeking the source of this magical music.

As I entered, the music intensified, reverberating around the single room and spiralling up to the vaulted ceiling.

It took away all my worries and left me with peace, even my broken heart felt mended under the caress of the chanting song.

I still couldn't make out the words or the singers, but in so many ways, it didn't even matter. It was sacred.

As the song built to a crescendo, I sank into a pew, unable to stand any longer.

Tears ran down my cheeks unbidden, as if all the sorrow I carried needed an outlet. I had never felt this close to my raw emotions, and I both welcomed and feared it.

It was too much, but I couldn't move. My body froze, desperate to get closer but also wanting to run away.

When the music stopped, I stayed in the pew for a long while, resting my head against the polished bench in front of me. I felt as if I'd finished a marathon weapons training session against a vampire. Drained and in need of food.

Chapter 29

I wandered the corridors until I found the large room set aside for eating. Six o'clock was early for a Mediterranean dinner, but several nuns sat waiting at their benches.

I chose a seat next to a young-looking nun with a lock of thick black hair peeking out from beneath her wimple.

"Is it OK if I sit here?"

She smiled and nodded.

"I'm not really sure of the protocol." I smiled back, but she didn't answer. "Do we wait for food, or do we have to go and get it?"

Another small smile. I frowned, worried that my Italian had worsened rather than improved after my stay with Marco's family.

The nun stood and walked to another table before sitting down. The elderly nun at her side – Sister Ursula – narrowed her eyes at me, making them disappear into her wrinkled face. My frown deepened. Was I not allowed to talk to nuns?

Sister Theresa entered, spotted me – it wasn't hard, I was the only one not in a dark habit – and sat down.

I smiled but she must have sensed my discomfort.

"Is everything well?"

"I think I offended someone." I glanced over my shoulder and Sister Theresa followed my gaze.

"Oh, that's Sister Benedetta. She has taken a vow of silence, apart from singing, but she finds it difficult to keep if we talk to her. She prefers to avoid temptation."

"Should I go and apologise?" Like an idiot, I had spoken to someone who had taken a vow of silence. I felt awful.

"No, how would you know?"

Fair point. Then something Theresa said jolted me and I stared after the nun with awe. "Was she the singer in the chapel earlier?"

Sister Theresa lowered her voice and leaned in, resting her elbows on the long wooden table. "She's a siren."

I did a double take. A siren. "Like the ones who used to lure sailors to the rocks?"

Sister Theresa laughed, causing several other nuns to turn in our direction as she hiccupped loudly in the comparative silence of the dining hall. She covered her mouth and go her shaking shoulders under control. "Do you believe everything you read? Sirens only killed those who came to hurt them."

"Sirens aren't my specialist area." I tried to keep my voice light, but it came out huffy. That hurt. I prided myself on my knowledge, and this merry nun had deflated me with one sentence. Of course, I didn't believe everything I read. I approached it all with a healthy dose of academic scepticism. I racked my brains for something to prove I was smart.

"Doesn't she need water?" Real smart, Aloora.

"I believe she swims in the lake."

"And you let her sing?"

"We all come to God in our own ways. Sister Benedetta has a wonderful voice that can lift the spirits of even the most mournful soul. Why would anyone deny her using her gift? She does no harm, and she harmonises like an angel."

Someone placed a basket of coarse bread in front of us. I took a piece and chewed, mulling over what Sister Theresa had said.

The Mother Superior stood and said Grace. I put the bread on my plate and swallowed surreptitiously, looking around at all the bent heads.

I had always thought nuns were stuffy do-gooders who would try to convert the unwary. I was prepared to debate the existence of God if the topic came up, but this simple tolerance snuck up on me and disarmed me more than any argument.

Sister Theresa spoke of celebration of differences instead of hiding them, a complete juxtaposition to what I always thought was the point of making everyone wear a baggy habit.

I ate the rest of the meal in silence, enjoying the simple fare after two weeks of feeding by Mamma Vegoia.

Soon enough, everyone finished, and the nuns disappeared off to wherever they went after eating.

I got up with no clear idea of where to go and my feet took me back to the chapel.

As I crossed the courtyard, a flash of movement outside the nunnery caught my eye. I stared hard at the trees, daring whatever was there to reveal itself.

A young deer hopped out of the undergrowth and darted away down the road.

I huffed a laugh. Frightened by a deer, what an idiot. But the feeling of unease didn't leave me as I headed into the chapel.

Chapter 30

It was a simple place; bare stone walls, wooden pews polished by the bums of countless nuns over the centuries. Stained glass windows cast colourful patterns onto the stone floor, and the only internal decoration was the fresco behind the altar.

A woman – another saint, judging by the golden halo around her head – sat cradling a dragon on their lap. A rare glimpse into the harmony that could occur when people, mundane or supernatural, worked with these magnificent animals instead of trying to kill them. Of course, she was a first century saint painted in the thirteenth century, so her clothes were wrong, and her face reflected ideals of beauty at that time, but the simplicity of her features and the calm, benevolent look on her face made my heart sing.

I felt she was a kindred spirit who recognised dragons, not as cruel beasts but as wonderful creatures who had much to teach us. And I knew that this was the exact right place for me to be right now.

I sat there contemplating her as the sun moved round, carving a coloured path across the chapel through the stained glass.

After a while, a swishing sound came from behind me and a gaggle – what was the collective noun for nuns? A holiness? – of nuns filed into the room, taking up the seats closer to the front. My eyes darted round, shaken from my introspection, and I screwed up my face as I considered leaving.

But that would be ruder than listening to their evening prayers, so I stayed in the pew, my back straight and body tense as I prepared to sit through a religious service.

I once joked to Amethyst that I couldn't spend any amount of time in a religious space because I might burst into flames. The Church – with a capital C – wasn't exactly welcoming to people who didn't fit their expectations, and religious zealots had been behind many a witch hunt, both figurative and literal.

But here, it felt like an older sort of religion, one more in touch with the loving aspects of scripture rather than fire and brimstone.

I listened to the service, chanted in Latin, and let my mind wander.

I gazed back at the painting and shook my head. In the fading light, she reminded me of a certain elf I had left behind, or rather, who had left me.

I braced myself for the gut punch that usually followed thinking of my ex, but there was only calmness. I didn't even resent her choice, but I hoped that Shesalva was happy and, although I wasn't content with it, I could try to find my way there.

One day in a nunnery and inner peace had found me. Inconceivable. In my experience, peace could only be found through study, preferably in a library, accompanied by an herbal tea. What magic did these nuns possess?

The chanting finished with a sweet song that spoke of heartbreak and healing, and tears streamed down my cheeks in an unbroken river.

I stayed there, gazing at that painted woman as the nuns left.

A voice broke the silence, making me jump. A nun had sat down beside me while I was caught up in contemplation of the painting.

"You are in love," Sister Theresa said.

I nodded and wiped away my tears with the sleeve of my stretchy dress.

"Is that why you are here?" When I started to protest, the nun gave me a look and said, "People who are satisfied with their lives do not come to live in a convent."

"It's part of the reason." I paused. "I do want to study dragons, too." Odd that dragons were the second thing that came to mind.

That's my problem. When I fall, I fall hard. So hard I slam into the ground heart first when it doesn't work out. But this was the hardest. I'd thought me and Shesalva were forever. I'd planned out our lives together, plotted everything out in my head while she had prepared to leave me.

"You run away instead of talking about your feelings." It wasn't a question.

I bristled. "She was the one who wanted a break." I inhaled sharply, expecting a rebuke from the religious nun at the revelation that my lover was a woman.

Instead, she looked me straight in the eye and asked, "And what do you want?"

"Love," I whispered like it was a prayer offered up in this sacred place.

"You cannot expect love if you do not first love yourself."

"How does a nun know so much about love?" I asked.

Sister Theresa smiled. "We experience it every day." My scepticism must have shown on my face, because she added, "Everyone thinks that because we choose a life of devotion, we do not experience the same emotions as everyone else. We choose to live apart from the world, but we still live in it. We are still people. And I have chosen my love of God above my love for all others, and They reward me by filling my heart with love."

"You're very wise."

Her bubbly laugh filled the chapel. Somehow, it wasn't a desecration of this quiet sanctuary, but a celebration of it. "So, what would you like to do?"

I inhaled a deep breath. That was the question. There were answers too big to give, so I focused on the reason I had come here.

"I would like to go to the library."

Chapter 31

I didn't get to the library until the next day. Sister Theresa insisted it was too late, and I needed sleep. She was right. Bells went off at ungodly hours of the night, or maybe they were godly hours, given where I was, but it was still far too early.

I woke several times, drifting back off, only to be woken again by the dainty pealing of the cursed – or should that be blessed? – bells. They were deliberately timed for maximum sleep deprivation and by the time it was properly morning, I was exhausted.

No wonder the nuns went to bed so early.

Sister Theresa knocked on my door, waking me for the final time that morning.

I opened it, peering through my slitted eyes. I took in the small basket she carried.

"Room service?" I raised an eyebrow. Well, I thought I did. My eyes were doing their own thing in protest at lack of sleep and wouldn't open fully.

"You missed breakfast," she said, coming in and placing the basket on the chair.

"What time is it?" I went for my phone, remembered I didn't have it with a shock that jolted me awake. It was like remembering that you had lost a hand.

"Gone nine o'clock."

Still early then.

I grunted a reply and removed the chequered cloth from the wicker basket, revealing some fruit and a slice of buttered bread.

There was another reason she was here, too. The library. My sluggish brain brightened as excitement flooded my veins. "Cool, I'm ready. Let's go."

Sister Theresa gave a small cough. "Do you want to get dressed first?"

I looked down at the oversized t-shirt that I wore as a nightdress. "Give me two minutes."

Dressed and munching on an apple, I followed Sister Theresa across the corridor to a building next to the church.

I pursed my lips. I'd expected a huge, ancient library and instead she led me to a small building with a non-descript door. I took a breath. There could still be priceless manuscripts inside.

As if sensing my disappointment, Sister Theresa turned as she got to the door and gave me a mischievous smile that contrasted with her nun's habit. "Welcome to the library."

Chapter 32

The door opened onto carved stone steps leading down. She paused to light a lantern that hung from a hook in the wall – old-fashioned but fitting – and waved me on. Guess I was going first.

Placing one hand on the rough wall and clutching my satchel tight against my body, I descended the stairs, fighting the sensation that the walls were closing in on me. I forced myself to inhale and exhale in a steady rhythm, telling myself that it was just a staircase, not a confined space, that I would be fine. Sister Theresa placed a reassuring hand on my shoulder, and I realised I had stopped. Another deep breath and I moved on.

The steps were uneven, with a slight depression in the centre of each stair that spoke of centuries of use.

Behind me, the soft footsteps of Sister Theresa followed me down into the colder air below ground. I shivered in my t-shirt, unused to coolness after the heat of the Italian summer. A prickle over my skin told me there was powerful magic somewhere nearby, and the intensity grew as we descended.

The flicker of Sister Theresa's lantern on the carved walls made me feel like we had gone back in time to a different age with every step.

After several turns of the spiral, a door appeared.

"Our library," Sister Theresa said, motioning me to descend another couple of steps so she could unlock it with a large iron key.

"What's down there?" I peered into the gloom of the continuing spiral where my gnome senses told me there was strong, ancient magic waiting in the dark.

"Our most precious treasure."

"More precious than books?"

"You tell me." She pushed the door, and it opened without a sound. Sister Theresa motioned for me to go in and stepped back.

I climbed back up the couple of steps and entered the room.

I gasped. It was beautiful.

Soft crystal lights hung on the walls, illuminating shelf after shelf of scrolls and bound books that stretched on under the entire abbey.

The scent of old paper and learning engulfed me like a blanket. Libraries were the one enclosed space I didn't mind. Maybe it was because each book contained its own world, somewhere I could escape to when everything else closed in on me.

I stepped forward and ran my hand across a smooth wooden table that already had several manuscripts on it.

"I retrieved some of our clearest references of Draconic for you, and you're welcome to read any document here." Sister Theresa held up a pair of white gloves. "We ask that you do not remove anything from the library and that you use these to handle the texts. These books," she tapped several large volumes, each half her height but slim and bound with a thick protective cover, "are our indices. We are in the process of digitising the library, but it is slow going and none of us are experts with technology."

"I might know someone who can help with that." There was a witch in the Cotswolds who had a cool program that created a virtual investigation board to go alongside Magical Liaison Office reports. And if she couldn't help build a database, then Maxi – our tech expert – could give it a go.

"Any help would be greatly appreciated." The sister beamed at me.

I took out a bottle of water.

"And no food or drink. Some of these texts are the only copies we know of in the world. We work to protect them through climate and lighting control and by avoiding unnecessary risks."

"Like food and drink."

"Exactly."

I put the bottle away. I could respect the desire to protect knowledge, and, while I wasn't clumsy, accidents could happen.

"I'll leave you to it. Let me know if you need anything." Sister Theresa pressed the cool iron key into my palm and left me alone in the sanctuary of knowledge.

My shoulders fell. Spaces like these were where I felt most at home. A safe retreat from the world when people let me down or shut me out. No book resented me or held their covers closed through spite.

I opened up my laptop and pulled the first manuscript closer to study the tiny text.

Chapter 33

I lost days in a new rhythm of waking at a normal time – the bells soon stopped bothering me and I reverted to my preferred habit of getting up mid-morning – jogging around the complex before it got too warm, walking to the library and studying until dinner time then enjoying a meal with Sister Theresa before retreating to my room, charging my laptop and working on my thesis until the early hours of the morning.

It was bliss.

On the tenth day, I realised I hadn't reached for my phone once. There was something freeing about not having a connection with the outside world.

If I needed something, I had to rely on my notebook, or what I'd already downloaded onto my laptop, or the library.

And so, I lost days to perusing the library, savouring the feel of ancient paper against my gloved hands and the musty smell of learning that accompanied every book I opened.

I discovered an original incantation written by Saint Silvestro himself about putting a dragon to sleep using its true name next to musings on the glory of God. In another book, I found conjugations of Draconic verbs scribbled alongside Latin. Yet another was filled with tales of times when dragons roamed and how saints had defeated them. They were retellings of earlier, lost texts, interpreted through the authors' time and biases, but still as close to primary evidence as I could get.

I copied them all down, even snippets of psalms and sonnets from Saint Silvestro's journal itself, or a copy of it, anyway.

I jotted down texts that had stayed hidden from scholars for centuries and made connections, feeling like a medieval scribe as I scrawled down the references and my thoughts.

It felt natural to copy things into my notebook and mind map the central arguments for my thesis before transferring it to the laptop in an outpouring of text that had escaped me back home.

In less than two weeks, I had made more progress than I had in a decade. The end was in sight. And every day a new discovery waited for me, enriching my research and giving me a new angle, as if the library wanted me to unlock its knowledge.

With this contentment, I don't know what impish thought made me descend the stairs that morning.

I had finished my breakfast of fruit, enjoying the lighter fare that the nuns lived by and feeling healthy now Mamma Vegoia wasn't handing me pastries every day – they were delicious but not good for me – when I paused at the door to the library and swung my lantern over the steps that carried on down into the darkness.

A sudden desire to carry on down came over me. I fingered the necklace at my throat and bit my lip as I considered following the steps down deeper underground.

I glanced up. No one was there. The nuns had left me alone to do my research, trusting that I was a kindred soul who wouldn't hurt their library. I don't know why I expected one to charge down the stairs wielding a weapon and maybe a bible to berate me for trespassing.

If I went down, I could take a peek at what was there. Most likely there would be another heavy door and I didn't have a key, so I'd return to the library.

That decided it. It was a fool's errand, but I had made so much progress with my thesis, I could spare a few minutes to investigate a little. And I could always turn back.

Plus, Sister Theresa had never told me not to go down there…and climbing up and down stairs was a good workout. Agent Jones, my boss, would not be happy if I came back out of shape after a summer off.

I was already around the first turn in the spiral before I'd finished internally rationalising my descent. And as I'd started, I decided to carry on, my natural curiosity easily quashing any arguments that came to me.

The lantern flickered on the soft orange stone of the walls, and I trailed one hand against the carved rock, the rough stone warm beneath my fingertips despite being so far underground.

A spiderweb tangled in my hair and on my neck. I brushed it away, crashing against the wall and falling a couple of steps in my panic.

This was a bad idea. I shouldn't be here. But it couldn't be much further. I waited for my breathing to settle, reminding myself I wasn't trapped, telling myself that my racing heart was excitement rather than panic until my legs stopped trembling and I could move on.

I held the lantern higher and dodged my way past more cobwebs as I continued to descend.

A tingling sensation passed through my body, and I shivered at the contact with magic, but didn't pause.

The temperature stayed consistent as the stairs wound down. A small part of my brain marked that as odd, that it was normally cooler the deeper underground you went, but I paid it no heed.

The sensation of magic grew as I descended, overwhelming me until it felt like my skin crawled with ants. Whatever this was, it was powerful, but I couldn't stop myself. Curiosity killed the cat and, judging by the power emanating in almost tangible waves up the stairs, it might kill me, too. I readied my knife for the comfort of having a blade in my hand. Metal wouldn't do anything against most spells, but it was reassuring to be armed.

As I rounded the final turn, I froze.

There, in an open cavern, lay a dragon.

Chapter 34

I hesitated on the bottom step, blinking to make sure I was awake.

But this was no delusion. There, in the centre of a gigantic cavern lit by some sort of glowing lichen, a red dragon lay sleeping under the abbey. I screwed up my face. No, not under the convent, outside it. If my calculations were right, but I hadn't kept count of the turns in the staircase.

The necklace at my throat heated, as it always did in the presence of dragons. I rubbed the large scale between my fingers, the smooth feel of it calming me.

I stepped forward and paused, half expecting the floor to tremble and wake it. Instead, a multitude of small crystal lights flickered on, illuminating the cave.

The walls were bare, apart from the crystals embedded there. I peered up at the nearest one, admiring the dwarven craftmanship that went into such a seamless join with the wall.

A narrow stream wound past the dragon, its rushing water echoing pleasantly around the cave.

I crossed the small stone bridge, holding my breath as I got closer to the dragon.

Its chest moved in and out in a barely perceptible motion and its hot breath moved my hair as I approached.

Someone, or many someones, had placed small votive items around it. Jewellery, gold, rolled up pieces of paper littered the floor on its side of the stream.

I picked up one of the pieces of paper and unfurled it. It read:

Grant me the peace to choose my path. I am so conflicted in my calling. Should I choose God or Luca? Give me the wisdom to make the right choice.

It was signed with a T. Theresa? I placed it back and selected another. This one was older and talked of the terror of the war, asking for protection against the wailing bombs. The sisters here had petitioned the dragon for centuries.

Not a big leap from petitioning a god. Except you could see the dragon.

I approached it, taking the time to appreciate its majestic form. Despite studying the dragons at Breconia – the elven nature reserve where they resided – and riding Fulgor, their beauty and power never ceased to capture me.

This one was smaller than my blue friend and had a pointier nose and larger frill behind its head. Its red scales were almost luminescent in the soft light.

I reached out and stroked one scale with the back of my finger. It was warm to touch and smooth against my skin.

It was criminal that these beautiful creatures left the skies, forced into slumber by magic users after they turned against humans and magical beings alike. Or, more accurately, after supernaturals and mundanes had turned against them. It depended on which contradictory accounts you believed, and no one knew exactly when the last dragon had disappeared.

Either way, they had faded from memory, nothing more than fairy stories or plot points in fantasy novels until more recent times when they had awakened, along with all the old prejudices.

The dragon scale in my necklace heated against my skin.

In my mind, I heard the magnificent creature speak in the rasping tones of Draconic. *Who are you?*

I backed up a step, my heart racing. Its eyes remained shut, its breathing steady. No dragon aside from Fulgor had spoken in my mind.

I opened my mouth to answer. A hand clamped down on my shoulder.

Chapter 35

I jumped and let out a surprised scream instead.

I whirled, ready to fight. And faced the forbidding stare of Sister Ursula, the nun who had glared at me when I first arrived.

"What are you doing here?"

"I…er…" I didn't have a good answer. "I'm sorry. I was curious."

"Too much curiosity means the bird is caught in the net."

I frowned at the Italian proverb before I understood; curiosity killed the cat.

"Sorry." It was all I could say.

"Come with me." Sister Ursula pulled me along. Her bony hand dug into my arm as she dragged me back across the bridge and out of the room.

As we left, the lights dimmed, leaving the dragon to its peaceful slumber.

Sister Ursula pushed me in front of her as we entered the spiral staircase, her long fingers prodding my back if I dawdled as we climbed back up.

I paused at the library door. Maybe she'd let me go back to my studies.

No such luck. Another prod and I continued the climb until we were back in the harsh light of day. I blinked at the sudden brightness.

Sister Ursula snatched the lantern from my hand and hung it on the hook before pushing me across the cobbled courtyard to the Mother Superior's office.

The Mother Superior was busy speaking to two other nuns – the siren Sister Benedetta and Sister Theresa – but Sister Ursula interrupted with rapid Italian.

I got the gist. An outsider had seen the dragon. This couldn't stand. They should force me out.

I hung my head. I had blown my chance to finish my thesis because of my curiosity and desire to know more.

But, as I thought back to the slumbering dragon and its raw powerful beauty, I knew I wouldn't give up that experience for anything.

I snapped out of my thoughts to see the Mother Superior gazing at me with bright eyes. She dismissed Sister Benedetta and sat down in the large chair behind her plain desk.

The Mother Superior gestured for me to sit, too. Sister Ursula hovered behind me like a goon in a mafia movie while Sister Theresa wrung her hands together and stayed near my side.

The Mother Superior steepled her fingers and gave me a
level look. "This is a problem."

Chapter 36

I leaned forward. "I know, I'm sorry–"

She held up her hand to stop my speech. "You have seen something that our order has worked hard to protect over many centuries since Saint Silvestro founded this abbey."

"We must ensure her silence." Behind me, I swear Sister Ursula cracked her knuckles.

Sister Theresa placed her hand on my shoulder. "There's no need for drastic measures. Aloora is like us." I squirmed in a seat. I was practically the opposite of a nun. "She cares for dragons. You read her letter of application. It was enough for you to grant her access to our archives."

The Mother Superior's face softened, and she reached into a drawer, pulling out a familiar letter with my signature at the bottom. With hindsight, the doodle of a dragon underneath my name had been a mistake. "Yes, your letter moved me, I must confess. Your interest in learning to better communicate with the dragons who share our world and to foster relationships with them that aren't based on violence is a noble goal."

I nodded along to my own words paraphrased back at me. "I am so sorry, I should never–"

"The fault is mine," Sister Theresa announced, stiffening at my side.

I gaped up at Sister Theresa, standing at my shoulder like an angel, with the sinister Sister Ursula glowering on my opposite side.

"I told her that we kept our greatest treasure down those stairs, but did not forbid her from seeking it. I take full blame."

"Then she must be punished." Sister Ursula's voice was hard.

"No! She shouldn't have to take the punishment for my actions." I jumped up.

"Sit down." The Mother Superior waved me back to my seat. She steepled her fingers again. "What will you do with this knowledge?"

I swallowed. "I won't tell anyone. I can keep your secret. I work for a government organisation, the things I've seen that no one would believe could fill a book."

"I need your oath."

I raised my hand. "I swear it."

"In blood."

"Is that really necessary?" Sister Theresa tried to intervene but a sharp look from her leader quashed her protest. She placed a hand on my shoulder in sympathy.

I inhaled sharply. Blood oaths were rare. I didn't know much about them, but if you broke one, you died. It was simple. Any sophisticated magic involving blood usually invoked death somehow, that was why it was considered dangerous. "May I finish my studies as planned?"

I didn't have anything to lose, so I might as well negotiate.

Sister Ursula sucked in a breath, but the Mother Superior spoke before she had a chance. "If you take the oath, it will be as if nothing happened. There will be no need for you to leave until your scheduled departure date."

The unspoken threat hung over me. If I didn't swear, they'd throw me out…and maybe do worse things to me. The Catholic Church's record with people who were a threat wasn't exactly rosy.

"I'll swear."

Chapter 37

The Mother Superior nodded and retrieved a sharp knife with the handle shaped like a cross from another drawer. I stared at its silver blade.

Sister Ursula's hand clutched my shoulder, pressing me into my seat as if I'd even think of leaving.

Power gathered in the Mother Superior's hand and my skin itched in the presence of her magic. I focused on the glistening knife as she pricked her finger and allowed a drop of her blood to coat the blade.

It was only later that I thought it was weird that a witch headed up a convent of nuns.

The Mother Superior met my gaze. "Aloora Neebly who goes by Dragonquest, do you swear to keep the dragon that rests beneath this convent a secret with your life as forfeit if you reveal its existence?"

Short but clear.

Sweat trickled down my back, and I swallowed to get some moisture back in my dry mouth before I croaked, "I do."

"Your blood for your life."

I held out my hand. The Mother Superior supported my wrist to stop my trembling. I was trained in combat, taught to face weapons without showing fear, but this was different. My access to the library was at stake. I screwed up my face, anticipating pain as she brought the knife towards my skin.

The point pierced my finger and the Mother Superior waited until a large drop of blood swelled from the tiny cut before she ran the flat of the blade through my blood, coating it.

The magic snapped over my body with an uncomfortable twinge that made me shudder and left a metallic taste in my mouth.

The Mother Superior nodded and wiped the knife clean with a handkerchief, her magic dissipating as quickly as it had appeared.

She placed the blade back in the drawer and rested her hands on her desk. "There. That's done."

"And the punishment?" asked Sister Ursula.

"Ah, yes…"

"Hang on, I took your oath."

"Not for you." Sister Ursula glared at Sister Theresa.

The Mother Superior tapped a finger against the table. "Sister Theresa, you disclosed the location of our greatest treasure to an outsider, threatening the safety of our order and the dragon in our care."

Sister Theresa stood pale and upright as she faced the Mother Superior.

"Therefore, I shall choose a punishment that fits your disobedience."

Sister Ursula leaned forward, hanging off every word.

"You shall accompany Aloora as she finishes her research, escorting her to and from the library at all times. And you shall eat with her and show her any treasures she wishes while she is here."

Sister Theresa nodded, accepting her punishment.

"That's it?" Sister Ursula asked, her fingers digging into my shoulder like claws.

"Is there a problem, Sister?" the Mother Superior asked, raising one eyebrow. "As penance for not watching our guest, she must now watch her whenever she is out of her room. Do you disagree that it is fair?"

"No, Mother Superior." Sister Ursula hung her head and released her grip.

"Then you are all dismissed. I have much to do." The Mother Superior bent her head over some paperwork, ignoring us.

I met Sister Theresa's gaze. She nodded. I took that as my cue to leave and followed the nuns out of the Mother Superior's office.

Chapter 38

Sister Ursula stalked off without a backwards glance, using her cane to propel herself along with smart taps on the tiles.

Sister Theresa set off in the other direction, and I trailed after her. I wanted to talk but didn't know what to say, so we walked in silence to the chapel.

I didn't even pause before entering. I found myself drawn here. Maybe it was the peace, or the stained-glass window, or the chanting, or the picture that reminded me of a certain elf, but it felt right.

Was I considering becoming a nun? I pinched myself. No. I still didn't believe in a deity.

I don't consider myself to be a religious person. I rely on books and research rather than an almighty power. I've never prayed and the only thing I've ever tried to communicate with that I couldn't see was dragons, before they came back into the world, but they'd turned out to be real.

But there was something about the peacefulness here, how everyone seemed so calm within themselves that felt, if not godly, then otherworldly. As if I'd stepped into a more spiritual realm that radiated utter calm and assurance.

Sister Theresa sat down in a pew, made the sign of the cross and bent her head in prayer.

I slumped next to her and wrapped my arms around my torso to stop me from fidgeting as I waited for her to finish.

While she prayed, I gazed at the fresco of the woman with the dragon. It was pathetic that it reminded me of Shesalva still. Even with all I'd accomplished here and the amazing dragon I had witnessed, she still snuck into my thoughts.

I tore my gaze away to find Sister Theresa studying me. "So, you found our dragon."

"I really am sorry…"

"What took you so long?"

"What?"

She sighed and leaned back against the hard pew. "It is rare for an outsider to be allowed in our library. I see your necklace – a dragon scale – and I read your letter and some of your work online. You seek harmony between the species, something which Saint Silvestro himself worked for. You've read his writings."

"How did you get online?" She had been adamant about me giving up my phone.

"He could communicate with dragons too, you know." Sister Theresa ignored my question.

I nodded. I had read some of his journals and his command of Draconic was impressive, as was his way of writing it down to preserve the knowledge.

"It saddened him, but when he realised people would still come to kill our dragon, he placed it into a deep sleep until a better time. They both agreed it was the best thing to do."

"And I've endangered you all."

"Not if you say nothing. I thought you would understand and, if you do achieve an understanding between dragons and other species, I wanted you to know that our dragon was here. The poor thing has been asleep for centuries. It must be so lonely…I'd like to give him, or her, a chance at life, if I can."

"Thank you," I whispered. She had shown more trust in me than I deserved. That in itself was a rare and precious gift. One I wasn't worthy of.

She tilted her head to one side, considering me. "Why do you think you are unworthy?"

I stared at her. I hadn't spoken aloud. Did nuns have psychic powers?

Sister Theresa laughed, her coughing hiccups echoing around the chapel. "Don't look at me like that. It is easy to see your thoughts on your face. Do you want to talk?"

"I just…you trust me with so much when no one else has."

She stayed silent.

"It means so much that you've welcomed me when I'm never good enough."

I gazed down at my feet, ashamed that I'd overshared. Dzraking nun superpowers.

Sister Theresa placed her hand on my arm and waited until I raised my gaze. "You are enough."

"Then why does everyone reject me? My parents when they found out I was gay, Lilith when I told her I wouldn't let her plagiarise my work for her grades, and now Shesalva. I opened up my heart to her, and she needs a break."

"And so, you feel she rejected you, too."

"She did reject me. She said she needed a break. That's pretty clear. I don't know how long you've been a nun, but that's code for breaking up. There was a whole series of Friends about it." I sighed. "It's what always happens, I do something to scare them off and they leave… Or they take advantage of me. When I'm in, I'm all in."

"That sounds intense."

"It is."

"What if she really needed some space to think?"

I opened my mouth, then closed it again. This was a new and dangerous possibility; that Shesalva did still care for me, that I wasn't doomed to be alone forever, that she had been honest with me and just needed time. I had no response to the question. I had thought I was at peace with Shesalva leaving me and could move on, but now my heart swirled like it was caught in a maelstrom. What if I'd stayed and listened when Shesalva tried to talk to me in Breconia?

"Perhaps you should stop running from your life and instead face it."

I worked my jaw, not knowing what to say as the nun called me out. That was exactly what I'd done. I'd run from my relationship at the first hint of difficulty instead of being honest about how much I wanted it to work. I'd put off finishing my PhD until now because I was scared of the unknown, what would happen when I finally completed my thesis. The only reason I was here, working on it was because I was running from my feelings about Shesalva.

"I will pray for you."

I snorted without thinking, then felt my cheeks flush as my brain realised where I was. Sister Theresa smiled back at me with that Mona Lisa smile that meant I couldn't tell what she really thought.

"Thank you," I said, and I meant it. I might not believe in an Almighty God, but she did and, given the mess of my feelings for Shesalva and the work I needed to do on my thesis, I could use all the help I could get, whether it came from this world or another plane.

Chapter 39

Back in my room a couple of days later, I swore before looking around guiltily. There was something wrong about using foul language in a sacred space. But I'd left my notebook in the library, distracted by Sister Theresa calling me to dinner.

I huffed out a sigh. I needed some translations for the next part of my thesis, and I was making such good progress that I wanted to press on. I checked the time on my laptop clock, but the bells ringing in my ears told me it was Compline, the evening service that marked the end of the day.

Weighing up my options, I decided to walk to the chapel and meet Sister Theresa. Since the Mother Superior's decree, I couldn't go to the library, or anywhere without her. Technically, I shouldn't even leave my room, but how else was I supposed to find her?

I saved my work and closed my laptop with a snap. Shrugging on the single zip-up hoody I'd brought with me against the chill evening air, I made my way along the corridor to the courtyard.

Something niggled at the back of my brain. It wasn't until I stepped out into the open space in the middle of the complex that I could pinpoint it.

There was no singing. No chanting. Nothing. Just the empty, hollow tweeting of a few birds yet to roost.

The crawling sensation I recognised from Rome spread over my skin. I whirled round, trying to pinpoint the source.

A figure stepped out from the shadows by the gate.

Chapter 40

"Hello Aloora Dragonquest."

"Hello?" I looked around. There were no nuns in sight, and this man spoke English. And he knew my name. "Are you looking for one of the sisters?" It was worth a shot.

He laughed. It was shrill and forced. "I'm looking for you. I'm a big fan. It's Han."

"OK…"

"We've spoken before."

I frowned. I did not remember this freckled man. "I'm sorry…"

"It's me! We've discussed theories about why dragons left the world. My avatar is a red dragon."

My face must have stayed blank because he sighed.

"My handle is BigDragonEnergy."

"Oh." Yeah, I remembered him. He had some weird conspiracy ideas, but then a lot of my followers did. That was why I had set up my channels in the first place; to educate.

"And you're here in Italy."

"Yeah. It was tricky to find you." He wagged his finger at me. "I spotted you a couple of times in Rome but couldn't bring myself to talk to you. I was star struck. Can you believe it?"

"No." I couldn't believe it. I wasn't threatening at all. That was what made me a good MLO officer. No one saw a purple-haired gnome as a threat until I'd got close enough to subdue them.

"Anyway, our conversation needs to be private, so I followed you out of Rome–"

"You were in the black sedan?" He didn't match my expectations of men in dark glasses who chased innocent women. I mean, he did have sunglasses, but the socks and sandals look he sported weren't exactly Men In Black.

"Yes!" His face split into a broad grin and he held out his hand in a fist bump. I stared at it until he lowered his fist. "I wanted to talk to you, but then you turned off and I lost you. I didn't know you could drive like that."

"I don't put everything about myself online." But given this bloke had found me and wanted a one on one, I needed to reassess how much I did post.

"Sensible. Your driving made me realise I'd underestimated you. So, I went back through all your posts and my own research, and I found a few places to the north of Rome where you might be headed."

I raised an eyebrow. This was serious stalking.

"And here you are. At the convent of dragons."

"It's the Abbey of Saint Silvestro, and I'm not sure they allow men on the grounds." That was the whole point of being a nun, right? To avoid men.

"Did you know that they have a dragon here?"

My heart skipped a beat. How could he know that? I had found it through curiosity and access to their library. Sister Theresa had said it was their most previous treasure, one that they guarded with wards. So how had this internet conspiracy theorist found out about it?

"Do they?"

"Don't play dumb. You must know. Why else would you come here?"

"I'm writing my thesis–"

"Yeah right." His tone said he didn't believe me. "And you expect me to believe you don't know about the dragon?"

"What dragon?" I couldn't tell him, even if I wanted to. That was the point of a blood oath. Even now I could feel it snaking around my heart, ready to end me if I breathed a word about the dragon.

"This is dragon central in Italy." He raised his fingers and counted off his evidence. "There are several documented sightings of a slumbering creature underground. Caxton refers to it in his translation of the life of Saint Sylvester – the anglicisation of Silvestro." As if I didn't know that. "Then there's the unexplained disappearance of a group of children in the eighteen hundreds. And finally, a letter that one nun wrote to her family in the fifties than mentioned caring for a sleeping dragon." He gave me a smirk that said that settled it.

"What letter?" I asked, frowning. It was unusual that someone had a piece of research on dragons that I didn't.

"Someone posted it online when the first dragons were awakened. I thought you knew. Isn't that why you're here?"

"I'm here to finish my thesis on Draconic. I'm not searching for dragons." That was true.

"No. You already have one. I know there's a dragon here. And I want it."

Chapter 41

I recovered some of my senses and narrowed my eyes. "Dragons aren't things you can own."

"I've seen you ride one."

Curse my online videos. There were several of me and Fulgor as we flew over the Welsh hills, both revelling in the freedom and exhilaration of flight.

"That's different."

"How?"

"Fulgor and I have an…understanding."

"That's all I want. And look…" he reached into his pocket.

My heart ratcheted up a notch. I took a step back, raising my hands in a gesture of surrender. Too far away to fight him and not magic enough to do anything if he pulled a gun.

He drew out a small, dog-eared book and my breathing returned to something more normal.

"See, I've studied, just like you. And now we can work together. There's an enchantment to wake them, reverse the sleeping spell."

"I don't think that's a good idea."

His face crinkled in confusion. "But don't you want dragons in the world? I've seen your channel."

"I…" I didn't have a reply. I loved dragons and yes, I looked forward to the day when humans and dragons could live harmoniously, but we weren't there yet.

The dragons in Cardiff had been driven out by the army and forced to find refuge in an elven sanctuary. And my friend, Fulgor, had spent years enslaved to Mordred before I freed him.

No, there was a reason dragons slumbered. People couldn't deal with someone higher up than them in the food chain, so magic users put them into hibernation. From what I could understand from the garbled snippets of truth weaved into the legends, some went more willingly than others.

"I knew you'd be excited."

"No." I found my voice.

His eyes flashed. "I need your help. The incantation is in Draconic."

Of course it was.

"Even if you have a spell, it takes serious magic to wake a dragon."

Han's smile was manic. "I've got that covered. I just need help with pronunciation."

"I can't." I wouldn't.

"You will." And he drew a gun from another pocket.

Chapter 42

If I had my knives, maybe I'd stand a chance. I could throw them almost as well as Agent Jones. But I'd grown slack after three short weeks at the abbey with no threats. I'd even left my bracelet in my room, lulled by the sanctuary offered by the nuns. Stupid.

And, as the logical part of my brain kicked in, it insisted that knives weren't any good in a gun fight anyhow.

I let out a stream of curse words under my breath as Han gestured for me to walk ahead of him. He directed me while keeping up a stream of one-sided conversation as we went.

Fragments broke through my churning mind as I tried to think my way out of this.

"...such a big fan...can't believe we're working together...was worried when you stopped posting, before I figured it out...you'll be glad in the end..."

I rubbed my temples. It was amazing how muddy your thoughts can become when someone's threatening you with a gun.

He marched us up a hillock behind the chapel, and my heart sank. I did some muzzy mental arithmetic and, yes, this could be above where the dragon slept. Another curse left my lips, this time in Draconic. Something about tearing out his heart. Their curses were always so visceral.

"Yes, that's it. I knew you'd get on board." Han smirked.

Dzrak it. I switched back to Dwarfish, even in my mind.

He stepped closer, the sweaty heat of him invading my personal space. The cold barrel of the gun pressed up against my back.

With his other hand, he held his notebook open and showed me the phrase.

"This is all we need to speak, and they'll be another glorious dragon in the world." He read it out.

I winced at his poor pronunciation.

Draconic is a language designed for those with a mouth full of teeth and a penchant for death metal. He didn't even come close.

But I still held my breath. Nothing. Not a rumble. That didn't deter him.

"Now, I need help with the Draconic. I know it's got nuances." He tried again.

This time, he managed to say something about 'washing a fish'.

I relaxed a little. At this rate, the worst he could do was waste my time until I could figure out how to escape.

"You say it." He thrust the book up in my face.

I read the text, inserting a couple of deliberate mistakes.

His face twisted, and he looked from me to the book. "Are you sure?"

I nodded.

The gun dug into my back.

"That's it."

"We'll see." He stepped back and nudged me with the gun. I trudged forward to the small copse of trees that crested the hill, shivering as we passed into the shade, my wet t-shirt clinging to my skin, damp from the terror sweat that trickled down my back.

He directed us to a tiny clearing, and I froze. There, tied up on the ground, were the sisters of San Silvestro.

Chapter 43

Sister Theresa blinked up at me from the ground while Sister Ursula glared. Their Mother Superior lay unconscious on the floor, her head cradled in a nun's lap. An ugly lump swelled near her eye. The dzraker had hit a nun.

"Say it again," Han said, moving away from me and pointing the gun at the defenceless nuns.

"Don't hurt them. They don't know anything."

"They kept the dragon here, asleep against its will." He smiled at me, enhancing the crazy look in his eyes. "But I don't want to hurt anyone. I just want the dragon. So, say the phrase again."

He tossed the notebook at my feet. I bent to retrieve it, considering my options. I could keep up my pretence and risk the lives of the sisters who had taken me in and allowed me to study with them, or I could give him what he wanted.

Looking at the poor sisters, bound and gagged on the dirt, it was an easy choice. He didn't have any magic, so saying the phrase was meaningless.

I read the words.

He cocked his head. "That sounded different to last time."

"Draconic isn't always an exact science. Sometimes I have to study for months to fully understand a text."

He narrowed his eyes. "Again."

I complied. This time, he repeated it back to me. Dzrak it. He had it syllable perfect.

Nothing happened. I met Sister Theresa's gaze, trying to tell her it would be alright without speaking a word. And if she did have a direct line to a deity, now would be the time to use it.

Han nodded and put the book away, repeating the phrase over and over like it was his personal mantra. Then he opened the drawstring bag slung over his shoulder.

The gun waved wildly as he dumped the contents on the ground. This was my chance. I tensed, ready to spring.

And froze as a skull thudded onto the ground.

Chapter 44

"You killed someone?" My voice was breathy.

Han looked from me to the skull, his brow wrinkled with confusion, then he laughed. "This. Oh no, this is a relic. You nuns should appreciate that." He waved the gun at the sisters. "It's the skull of Saint Silvestro."

The patron saint of the abbey. The saint – or wizard, depending on your view of the scriptures – who put the dragon to sleep and then built the convent over it to protect it.

The hairs on my arms rose and my fingers tingled. It was magic alright.

"Who better to help me raise this dragon than the one who forced it to sleep?" He stroked the yellowed bone before picking it up with one hand.

Not for the first time, I wished I had magic. Proper magic. Not just some sort of innate sense that came with being a gnome. I could find my way around any bookstore, and I could unearth hidden gems in my research. But actual magic? Nothing.

"What if it wants to sleep?"

He laughed again. "Oh, Aloora, I always liked your sense of humour. Now, I'll ask for the last time; will you help me?"

I shook my head.

Han let out a long sigh and pointed the gun at me. "Then sit over there with the nuns and stay out of my way." He gave me a look filled with disappointment as I sat down next to Sister Theresa, the dry grass pricking my legs. "I thought we were the same. But I guess you can't trust people you meet on the internet; you never know who they really are."

I placed an arm around the worried nun. I would get the sisters away while he mangled the incantation.

Han lifted the skull up and repeated the phrase I had given him. Dzrak it, but he pronounced it almost perfectly.

I worked at the knots around Sister Theresa's wrists, wishing I had one of my knives on me. With her hands free, Sister Theresa pulled her gag out and untied the ropes at her feet while I moved onto the next nun.

Han ignored us, concentrating on repeating the incantation over and over. Goosebumps rose on my arms as the magic built around him. The skull must be powerful to amplify the tiny amount of innate magic that the human possessed. Or maybe Saint Silvestro's magic stayed with him after death. There was a reason magic users burned their dead instead of keeping them for relics; so people couldn't use their body parts in spells.

Soon, all the sisters were free and gaping up at the glowing skull in Han's hand.

"Get out of here," I whispered. "I'll tackle him."

It wasn't a great plan. But it was all I had.

I didn't wait to see if the nuns listened and rushed Han, tackling him from the side and cushioning my face in his slightly pudgy belly.

The skull fell to the ground with a crunch, still emitting the yellowish light of magic. We followed.

Han took the brunt of the fall, his breath whistling out as he hit the dirt.

I sat up and wriggled to get a better hold on him.

Han elbowed me in the face, snapping my head back in an explosion of pain.

I lashed out, punching him in the throat.

My training had taught me to disable my opponent fast. When you fought magical beings like shifters and vampires, you had to get them down before they got you. And the neck punch was one of the most effective moves. Han was human. He didn't stand a chance.

His hands went to his neck, and he gasped for air, gaping at me with his dark eyes.

As I considered my next move, Sister Ursula thwacked him across the head with her staff.

I gaped up at her. She shrugged, unrepentant. Sister Theresa pulled her back before she could hit him again.

"I thought nuns weren't violent."

"You didn't see her when she found the villagers stealing from our vegetable garden." Sister Theresa shook her head.

I knew Ursula was strict, but assault? I didn't realise nuns were that mean. I pushed myself off Han and snatched up the glowing skull.

The warmth of magic flowed through me in a prickling sensation, like pins and needles all over my body. At my throat, the dragon scale necklace heated.

That couldn't be good.

The ground juddered beneath my feet. I shouted at the nuns to run and backed away, tucking the skull under my arm.

We made it to the base of the hill before the ground split open and the red dragon burst out into the air.

Chapter 45

The dragon spiralled high in the sky, stretching its wings out, as if testing its sudden freedom after centuries underground.

Its red wings glowed with the fire of the setting sun. Behind me, several nuns sank to their knees. I didn't blame them. It was awe-inspiring, in the truest sense of the word.

Circling above us, it looped around in exhilarating spurts of flight until it spied us, specks of black against the green grass and dirt.

It dipped down and landed, its wings sending a gust of air at us. I covered my eyes as grains of dust pummelled my skin.

You. I recognise you from my dreams.

Its voice manifested in my mind in slow, deep Draconic as it caught me with its golden eyes. At my throat, my necklace heated as the dragon scale worked its magic and aided my understanding.

I dropped the skull and walked forwards. This felt right. This was how it was meant to be. People and dragons communing and working together.

You woke me. Are you a descendent of Silvestro?

I bowed my head. "I am so sorry."

Young one, if I am awake, then the gulf between our species is closed. This is not a time of sorrow, but of rejoicing. How long have I slept?

"I'm sorry because we are not in that utopia, and it was not I who woke you."

The dragon stamped its feet, making the earth shudder. *Then why am I here?* it growled.

"You're speaking with it?" Sister Theresa asked from her knees.

Her voice attracted the dragon. *Who are these black-coated women?*

"These are the sisters who have dedicated their lives to guarding you and continuing Silvestro's legacy."

As I said the saint's name, the nuns crossed themselves again.

Then I thank them for their care.

I passed on the message as the red dragon inclined its head at the group of nuns.

But who woke me?

Before I could answer, a reedy voice piped up from behind me in broken Draconic. "I woke you."

I spun round.

Han stood there, clutching the skull I had dropped, which still oozed magic.

"You can understand the dragon?" I asked in disbelief. I had thought I was the only one who understood Draconic well enough to converse with the beautiful creatures, a feat which had become easier in a way I didn't quite understand thanks to my necklace.

Han smirked at me. "I told you. I've followed your work on dragons and Draconic. And this relic amplifies our bond. It's destiny."

I recognise your magic, little one. Are you a descendent of my friend, Silvestro?

"No, he's–" I started.

"I hold Saint Silvestro's skull in my palm. I am the one who awakened you." Han's voice grew in confidence as he spoke, his fingers gripping Silvestro's eye sockets like he held a bowling ball. "I charge you, dragon, that you are now bonded to me. We shall soar the skies together as in times of yore and you shall help me smite my enemies." That crazy glint was back in his eyes.

This is why you have broken my slumber?

Han nodded, the skull shaking in his hand.

Foolish human. Vengeance is not a good motive. And you are so young. What enemies could you have? I will not help you in this.

Han screwed up his face.

The dragon turned its head to me. *I can see why you are sorry, if this is what humans think of us. I shall return to my rest.*

I stepped forward and placed a hand on its warm snout. "I am so sorry."

The dragon bellowed out a roar of pain, twisting its head so fast it knocked me to the side.

I landed hard; the air knocked out of me. *What the dzrak was that?* I swore.

The dragon beat its wings clumsily and staggered up into the sky as golden drops of blood fell from its side. Han stood in a wide stance; his mouth twisted into a cruel grimace. He held a thin blade coated with dripping golden ichor. He had stabbed the dragon.

Chapter 46

"Dragon! With your blood and the magic of Saint Silvestro, I charge you to obey me." Han smeared the golden blood onto the skull, which shone brighter as the dragon's life force powered his magic. I hated blood magic. He muttered something else.

I frowned as I translated the words. Some sort of spell to control another being. Illegal. And stupid.

"What's happening?" the nuns chorused, gaping up at the dragon.

Magic pricked my skin like a thousand tiny needles. I scratched my arms and squinted at the sky. Could a human really control a dragon?

Mordred had controlled Fulgor through pain and cruelty, but this was something else.

"Nothing good," I murmured, my skin still crawling with the crackling invisible energy that filled the evening air. "Come on, let's go."

I hustled the nuns away, back to the abbey where they could find safety. The Mother Superior had regained consciousness and staggered alongside us, accepting the support of her sisters as they retreated.

Once I was sure they were back within the high walls of their sanctuary, I marched back up the hill and squared up to Han who stood gazing up at the dragon that twisted in the evening sky. I wasn't running away from this. "Stop it."

"I thought we could be friends, Aloora. But it's true what they say; you don't know who anyone really is online. If you're not with me, you're against me."

"Don't do anything you'll regret. Please, Han." I added his name to make a personal connection, just like they taught us in the MLO.

"Regret? I've got my own dragon to control. And unlike you, I can see the true possibilities."

So much for forging a connection and convincing him to stop. I tried again, using logic. "The only possibility here is pain and death. Put the skull down and end this. When the authorities come, I'll tell them you cooperated."

He frowned at me. "Authorities? How can you call anyone for help without phones?"

He twisted around and called for the dragon.

I held my breath. This was the big test. Would the red dragon listen?

The dragon swooped down, unleashing fire over the convent complex. It dragged its claws over the roof of the dormitory, sending tiles cascading to the ground.

As the nuns reached the arched entryway of the complex, the dragon swooped low and unleased fire from its huge maw, engulfing the chapel in flames.

The nuns screamed in panic. I shielded my face from the sudden heat.

"Back this way." The Mother Superior's voice sounded over the rushing blast.

I raced to help them, tearing down the hill in record time, leaping the mounds of earth that the dragon had pushed up when it broke out from its cave. The stained-glass window shattered and the painted fresco on the chapel wall disintegrated in the heat. Something tore in my heart, as if I'd lost Shesalva again.

I saw my phone glittering on the ground among the debris. A miracle. I snatched it up and dialled for help, my fingers automatically dialling Shesalva's number. She might not want me, but I still loved her – I'd learned her phone number by heart for dzrak's sake – and I needed to tell her.

As my brain woke up, I realised that she might be the best person to call anyway. Because she lived in Breconia, and that meant that she could ask the elves for help. But it didn't matter because she didn't answer.

I cursed and scrolled through my phonebook for the Magical Liaison Office number as we fled. They would help. I tripped and my phone fell to the ground. It had survived dragon fire and the destruction of the Mother Superior's office, so, of course, a three-foot fall to the floor was what cracked it. As the screen died, I swallowed.

No one was coming.

Beside me, the Mother Superior stopped and gaped up at the burning wreckage of the building. Then she whirled round, magic gathering in her hands.

"You've destroyed our home and turned our sweet dragon into a monster," she said in accented English.

Han stared at the abbey. A slow smile spread over his spotty face. "It worked…It actually worked."

"Where are my sisters going to live now?"

He shrugged, his gaze tracking the dragon flying overhead.

The Mother Superior's eyes flashed, and she sent a gust of hurricane force wind at the middle-aged man.

I hunched my shoulders, caught at the edge of the blast. The roaring of the storm filled my ears. A weather witch. Maybe we could stop this.

He raised his arm over his eyes and lifted the skull high. His mouth moved, but his words were lost in the roaring maelstrom.

The dragon twisted in the air and dived, aiming for the Mother Superior.

Chapter 47

I sprinted towards her, colliding with the senior nun just as the dragon snapped its jaws in the spot where her head had been.

At the impact, her magic dropped, and Han stood upright, free from the gale that had surrounded him.

I stumbled to my feet. "Alright, you made your point. No need to harm the nuns."

The rest of the sisters gathered round their injured leader.

"You saw her. She tried to hurt me," Han whined.

"You destroyed her home with a dragon."

"Yes…let's find out what else I can do." He didn't say anything, just gripped the glowing skull.

The dragon felt the magic and whipped round, landing on the already damaged chapel roof. The beams gave way under its weight and crashed down with a thunderous creak.

The red dragon beat its wings, the down draught putting out the larger flames as it regained its balance.

It prowled towards Han. *You dare to try to control me.*

"I think you should stop now," I told Han. "Maybe we can still get out of this alive."

Han redoubled his efforts, muttering words I couldn't quite make out.

The dragon opened its mouth, flames gathering in its throat, aiming it at Han. Its eyes dulled from gold to a paler yellow, as if a film covered them.

It turned to me.

"You don't have to do this." I tried to reason with the dragon in its mother tongue, but it was too late.

I yelled at the nuns to move. I wasn't running away from this. It was my job to protect non magic users from magic gone wrong. That was the role of the Magical Liaison Office. And I wouldn't let the magnificent dragon in front of me kill innocent people.

I nodded to the Mother Superior, now back on her feet, as we locked gazes. She returned my nod and herded her nuns along.

Just one problem. I was a tiny gnome with no magic. I needed a miracle.

For the first time in my life, I shot a silent prayer up to the universe, asking for a way to buy some time so the nuns could get away. Maybe the deity they believed in would step in to help people who had dedicated their lives to serving them.

I stepped closer to Han. If the dragon breathed fire, it would engulf us both.

The dragon opened its mouth, flames burning at the back of its throat.

"No!" Han shouted, all his concentration on the dragon. The threat of burning alive narrows your focus like that.

I dived forwards and knocked the skull out of his hand. It bounced on the cobbled stones and a couple of yellow teeth shook free from its jaw.

Our gazes met, and we both launched ourselves at the skull on the ground.

I got there first, grabbing the relic like a rugby ball and hugging it to my body as I stood.

Han glared up at me.

I held the skull high and willed it to channel what little magic I possessed. It did nothing. A useless lump of glowing bone in my hands. I didn't know any spells to channel its power, and I had no magic.

Frustrated, I yelled, "Stop!"

But the dragon's eyes were still glazed over, and it gathered fire in its gaping mouth.

Han kicked out, sweeping my legs from under me. The skull flew from my hands, landing near the burning abbey.

Han crawled towards it. I jumped to my feet.

The dragon loosed its fire, carrying out Han's order. I dived out of the stream of flames and huddled behind the wall, the smell of burning hair engulfing me.

Han was nearby, still going for the skull. I pushed myself up and sprinted for him, crouching low behind the wall.

He turned, and I punched him in the jaw, missing my signature throat punch by a few centimetres. His head flew back, but he came at me, aiming a blow at my face.

I dodged to one side and feinted a claw at his eyes, so he jerked back on instinct. While he was distracted, I kneed him in the privates.

He curled in on himself, wheezing.

I followed through with an uppercut to his jaw and a stomach punch that brought tears to his eyes.

I had trained with enough people stronger than me to know that I needed to make every blow count and get my opponent down fast, before they could take advantage of their heavier weight or greater muscle mass against my spindly frame.

In desperation, Han lunged for me. It took me by surprise, and I wasn't quick enough to dodge his attack.

He tackled me to the ground. The worst place for me to be; stuck under a crazy man.

I struggled under his weight, but I couldn't budge his bulk. His chest heaved as he sat on my stomach.

I pummelled his torso with my fists, but I didn't have the full force of my body to put behind the punches or the reach to get past his chest. He ignored my blows.

He looked down on me in triumph. He had me and he knew it. The cocht-wimble.

I flailed with my hands, seeking a rock or anything I could use to even the odds.

He made a fist and raised it.

My hand closed on a smooth piece of wood. Sister Ursula's cane. I gripped it. I had one chance.

As his eyes sparked with his imminent triumph, I bucked my hips, distracting him while I hit him upside the head with every ounce of strength I could muster behind the cane.

He blinked at me. Then toppled sideways in slow motion.

I wriggled free, pushing his prone body away from me. I never wanted to be under a man again. Gripping my new weapon, I checked his pulse.

He was still alive.

As I weighed up what to do next, the crunching of crushed bricks sounded loud in my ears.

The red dragon peered over the wall; its eyes still glazed.

I braced myself for a fiery death. If it had to end like this, at least I was standing up for what I believed in and protecting innocent lives. I would be a martyr to the desire to protect and promote peace between dragons and people. And I wasn't running. Not anymore.

The dragon's head snapped up, sensing something.

A dark shape in the sky grew larger and larger as it swooped down.

"Fulgor!"

Chapter 48

And who was that on his back?

As the blue dragon I knew so well flew closer, I could make out a willowy shape with flowing red hair and my mouth fell open.

I'd never indulged in a fantasy for a knight in shining armour to ride to the rescue, but that was before seeing Shesalva, her beautiful face screwed up in concentration and anger, leap off the back of a dragon while loosing an arrow at the red dragon that loomed over me. It turned out I liked my women the same way I liked my books; well-read and covered in leather.

My heart soared, beating so fast I thought it would escape my chest. She had come for me. She cared.

With a roar of anger, the red dragon took to the skies, launching itself at Fulgor, self-preservation driving it to destroy the larger threat and leave puny gnomes alone.

Shesalva ran to me, covering the ground at an astonishing speed and shoved me behind her taller frame before nocking another arrow.

"Wh–wh–?" I stammered, all power of speech leaving me.

"You haven't been online in weeks."

Thwuk. An arrow flew from her bow.

"I've been studying."

"Amethyst was worried."

My heart sank again. She had come out of some weird obligation to her elven prince's wife.

Thwuk. Another arrow.

"And Fulgor agreed something was wrong."

"You spoke to Fulgor?"

"I'm not as fluent in Draconic as you are, but we got by. So, we consulted a seer, who said you were in trouble."

"But you hate that type of magic."

The elf snorted out a huff of breath and shook her head. "It's so imprecise."

"So, you just decided to fly over from Wales on the words of some mystic?" I put my hands on my hips as my anger rose. What right did she have to come over here on a whim just to discard me again?

"And I was worried."

I froze. My heart stopped.

I opened my mouth. But the red dragon's roar put a stop to any words I might have spoken.

"Now is not the time," Shesalva said, aiming another arrow at the dragon. She was right. If we survived this, then we could talk.

Above us, the dragons twisted in battle, breaking apart only to clash again in a cacophony of scraping scales that clanged over their fearsome roars.

I stood there, gaping up at them.

It was beautiful but terrible and my heart sank to think that I was the cause of all this pain. I should never have let Han follow me here, I shouldn't have given him the correct pronunciation and I should have been able to stop him before it came to this.

Fulgor's larger size meant every blow he landed on the smaller red shook the other dragon and sent it hurling away.

But the smaller dragon was faster, more able to manoeuvre itself and it strove to avoid the head-on collisions by darting in spiralling zig zags and attacking Fulgor before zooming out of reach.

I cried out as it tore through the thinner membrane that stretched across Fulgor's right wing. He roared his pain and flapped to the ground, the damage making him clumsy.

Shesalva shot arrow after arrow as the red dived, preparing to attack its grounded foe.

I rushed over to Fulgor. "How can I help?" I garbled in Draconic.

He roared at me to get back and I dived for the cover of the smouldering chapel as the red came back in.

Sister Theresa hissed at me, and I joined the nuns where they cowered behind the altar.

"Can we get the red back to sleep?" I asked.

"We are praying."

"We need more than prayer…"

A shudder passed through the remains of the building as the dragons clashed outside.

My gaze lit on Sister Benedetta – the siren. "Does your magic work on dragons?"

She shrugged, keeping true to her vow of silence.

"Well, it's the only plan I've got. There's something about the incantation that soothed it to sleep in the first place. I read it in the library. If you can sing that combined with the magic of the skull, maybe it will work."

Sister Benedetta nodded.

"Where's the incantation?" Sister Theresa asked, her hand around her sister's shoulders, lending her support.

I had copied it down in my notebook. My hand reached for my satchel's usual place at my side, but I'd left it in my room. Another memory bubbled into my mind.

My notebook was in the library, where I'd left it. Dzrak. I'd have to go get it.

Chapter 49

Sister Theresa squeezed my hand as she passed over the iron key to the library. She believed in me, and I wouldn't let them down.

With a shout to the nuns to secure the skull, I raced to the destroyed library next to the chapel. By some miracle, the spiral steps were intact, although they now opened onto the heavens.

I sent a silent thought to Fulgor to stay safe. I didn't know how far our psychic connection went – we'd never tested it like this – but it was all I could do. The only way to help was to get my notebook.

I raced down the steps, taking them two at a time.

Above me, the ground rumbled with the growls of fighting dragons. Streaks of dust drifted down, coating my skin with a thin layer of dirt.

The light from the stairwell soon faded as I descended further and further down below the chapel. My chest heaved as I fought panic. My brain played out visions of the ceiling caving in on me. At least the dragon had destroyed part of the chapel so less weight would crush me. Every cloud had a silver lining.

I got to the library door and pressed my fingers against the wood, trying to find the keyhole in the dark. The key trembled in my hand as the muffled sounds of the fight echoed down the stairs.

As I pushed the door open, I shoved the above ground world from my mind; I had to focus on my notebook and the incantation we needed.

Around me, the crystal lights flickered on, their soft light illuminating the undamaged library.

A thump shook the room, and a trail of dust drifted down from the ceiling. It would be a crime if all this knowledge was destroyed.

I considered grabbing some manuscripts, but the key to preserving them lay in finding my research, not in pulling ancient tomes to the surface so they could be burned by dragonfire. And there, where I'd left it on the desk, was my notebook.

I seized it, the familiar worn leather and embossed dragon design smooth and comforting in my hand.

I flicked through the pages, speed reading at championship levels until I found the incantation that Saint Silvestro had written down when he spoke about putting the dragon to sleep.

A smile curved my lips. I had it. Wedging my thumb between the pages, I turned to race back upstairs when the ceiling began to shake.

I froze, gaping up at the arching stone above me. Dust poured down, coating the library and my clothes.

Cracks appeared, zigzagging through the dwarf-wrought chamber.

Time to go. I spun on my heels and headed to the door when the first chunk of ceiling fell, sending a cloud of choking dust across the room.

I hunched down, cradling the notebook to my chest as the library plunged into darkness. A splintering thud reverberated around the room.

As the dust cleared, the crystal lights flicked back on. The crash must have caused a temporary blip in their magic. I glanced around, expecting swathes of the library to have been destroyed.

An enormous piece of rock lay atop of the remains of the desk, but none of the shelves were damaged. A lucky strike.

I glanced up. The splits widened as dragons roared, their bellows dulled by the layers of ground above me. Fractured spiderwebs of cracks laced the ceiling. The overwhelming urge to save the books came over me, but there was nothing I could do down here.

My arms cramped where I'd cradled my notebook tight against me, and I loosened my grip. This was how I could save the books. I had to get back.

On my first step towards the door, the room rumbled, and another large portion of the roof collapsed. I dived to the side, mistimed my roll, and crashed into a bookcase.

Wincing, I squinted through the growing dust, powerless as the ceiling caved in.

I wriggled my way back from the cacophony of falling stones, deeper into the library's vault, using the shelving as a guide in the dark.

Coughing, I stretched my top, pulling it over the lower half of my face, giving my lungs and dry mouth some meagre protection.

There was a loud bang close by as something detached from the wall.

Books fell onto me, shaken from their shelves. That's irony for you. I could die down here, buried by the very books I treasured. I shrieked as a heavy tome with metal corners dinged off my arm.

After an age, the shaking stopped, and I risked opening my eyes. A dislodged crystal glowed weakly at my feet, shaken from its mount in the wall. I grabbed it and took in the devastation.

I got to my feet and banged my head against a fallen bookshelf. As the dust settled, I could see it had wedged itself against another, creating a small pyramid of shelter for me and the manuscripts that now covered me.

Half of the library ceiling had collapsed, and papers fluttered to the ground. As I watched, a pile of scrolls fell in a cascading landslide of knowledge until they came to rest in a heap next to a lopsided chair.

The reality of it hit me. The library had caved in. Over my exit. And, worse, books had been damaged.

I was going to die, trapped in a confined space, surrounded by books I hadn't had a chance to read. This was my own personal hell.

I wanted to scream, to rail against the unfairness of it all and I clenched my fists, clutching the crystal…and my notebook. I had everything I needed. I just had to escape. The leather covered book in my hand was a solid, reassuring presence. I had to get back up top. People needed me.

Chapter 50

I scanned the room, looking for anything that could help me. Above me was dirt. Around me was debris and scattered paper. I crept forwards in the direction where the doorway had stood.

My eyes misted at the hopelessness of it. There was no way I could move any of the large chunks of stone that barred my way. A tear tracked its way down my face, smudging the dirt.

I sneezed at the coolness of it, then frowned. Tears were hot. So, why did my wet face feel cold? A string of sneezes followed as if the first one had unlocked my nose's irritation at the assault of dust.

Holding the crystal aloft, I examined the rubble. There was a tiny gap through the debris near the top, barely big enough for a human to pass through.

But I wasn't human.

I removed my thumb from where it still marked the page and folded down the corner. It was painful to deface a page with a deliberate crease, but necessary. And it was only a notebook, not like a proper book. Telling myself that didn't make it better.

Stuffing the now dog-eared notebook under my top for safekeeping, I clambered up a bookcase that lay on a slant, sending silent apologies to the crushed books I stepped on as I climbed. It was sacrilegious, but the only way to prevent more damage was to get out of here. As if in protest, the pages shifted under my canvas shoes, and I clung onto the wooden shelves and pulled myself upwards.

At the top, I balanced on a large piece of fallen ceiling and studied the space I'd spotted from the ground.

A shaft of light beckoned me from the other side. A tunnel.

I squeezed my way through the small gap, for the first time in my life glad that I was a tiny gnome.

I inched forward, taking my time, pushing the crystal ahead of me. The small space suffocated me, claustrophobia stealing my breath and forcing me to take shallow pants as panic clutched my chest. I pushed away the thought that if something shifted, I would be crushed by tonnes of earth that hung above me like a dirty guillotine blade. But it kept coming back, filling my mind with fear.

I started chanting in Latin to force my breath to come out evenly.

Blood pounded in my ears, louder with every movement I made, until my rapid heartbeat consumed me. With every shallow breath, I wondered how much oxygen I had left, even though I could see light through the tunnel. But then, fear isn't rational.

Panic consumed me and my slow, measured inching gave way to frantic wriggling. I had to get out of this deathtrap.

My Latin song gave way to shallow breaths.

Kicking with my feet and scrabbling with my hands, I got through the tunnel and collapsed in the destroyed stairwell.

I pressed my hands to my thighs and ducked my head between my knees as my breathing returned to something more normal.

A breeze ruffled my hair, and I turned my tear-stained face up. That was my way out.

Still trembling from the adrenaline of pure fear, I half climbed, half crawled up what remained of the stairs towards the light and the welcome fresh air.

I crested the stairs like a zombie, coated with dirt, shuffling and swaying and groaning with the effort of scrambling up the spiral stairs.

But I had made it. I checked my top and breathed out a sigh of relief. And I had the notebook.

Back up top, Fulgor lay on the ground, snapping up at the red dragon as it dived in and raked his scales with sharp claws.

"Hold on," I whispered, clutching my notebook against my body.

I dashed to the chapel, expecting to see the nuns there waiting, but there was no one. More sandstone blocks littered the ground, sitting atop smashed pews. The crucifix that had held pride of place behind the altar lay on its side among shards of coloured glass.

An arm waved from behind a wall. I sprinted over, slaloming past collapsed pieces of brickwork and smoking walls.

An earth-shaking roar rang through my ears. I found another spurt of adrenaline from somewhere and made it to where the nuns huddled around the skull.

Sister Ursula sat on Han, who moaned weakly. The tough nun nodded to me, whacked him on the head and tapped her recovered cane on the ground.

I ignored the man. He had caused enough trouble and Sister Ursula would keep him in check.

"Do you have the incantation?" the Mother Superior asked.

I nodded and held out my book. It was in Latin. The standard language for spells since Roman times.

I placed my hand on the skull and read it aloud. Nothing happened. My innate abilities were too weak to power a spell.

The Mother Superior joined me. The hairs on my arms stuck up in goosepimples as her power flowed into the skull. She repeated the phrase.

I glanced at Sister Theresa, who kept watch over the wall. She shook her head. The red dragon was still awake.

Sister Benedetta joined us, placing her hand on the skull next to mine and adding her sweet voice to our spell, so it formed a lullaby.

I blinked as the overwhelming compulsion to sleep came over me. Some nuns keeled over on the spot, falling into slumber in an instant.

I fought it, telling myself that this was the same as fighting sleep when I was up against an essay deadline and the desire to curl up on the ground lessened.

Sister Theresa wobbled at the wall but stayed awake long enough to turn to me and shake her head again.

I knew dragons were powerful magical creatures, but to resist the combined power of a witch and a siren was awesome. How had Saint Silvestro put it to sleep in the first place?

"It's not working!" The Mother Superior stated the obvious.

I wracked my brains. "Its name." Of course. Any spell was a hundred times more powerful if it was focused on a specific person or thing, and for that, you had to name it.

The nuns who hadn't succumbed to the siren's spell stared at me.

"The incantation is missing a name. It's not directed at anything specific; that's why we're feeling its effects."

"I do not know its name," said the Mother Superior, "none of us do. That knowledge was not passed down."

"Aloora will know it." A soft voice came from behind me. Shesalva had such confidence in me, it almost tore my heart into pieces again.

"Just…give me a minute."

Everything rested on my research. I snatched my notebook back from the Mother Superior and took a moment to compose myself, telling my gnome research senses that we needed this name. I remembered reading it in a transcription of a diary. I could see the neat calligraphy swimming in front of my eyes, but the letters weren't clear enough for me to make out a name. I took a deep breath. If I had seen it once, I could find it again.

I flipped the pages, trusting my innate magic to help me. Of course, there was always the possibility that I hadn't copied it down, but that was an option I didn't want to contemplate.

I skimmed the pages, searching for anything that might help.

My gnome senses tingled as I flipped through the book until there, there, right in the middle of a treatise on paganism and the reverence of dragons that I'd jotted down some quotes from was the dragon's name.

Chapter 51

I had copied it down in the phonetic runes of written Draconic, so I repeated it for everyone, taking care over the syllables.

The nuns garbled it, sounding like they were doing impressions of monsters at a death metal gig, but then Draconic always sounded a bit like that.

A pained roar crashed over us.

The pronunciation was close enough.

I placed my hand back on the skull. The Mother Superior put hers on its bony cranium too, followed by Benedetta. Shesalva placed her cool hand over mine, sending sparks of intimacy off in my stomach that had nothing to do with magic. The other nuns who remained awake joined in too, until we all touched the artefact.

We repeated the spell, inserting the red dragon's name amid the flowing Latin.

Our combined magic flowed through me, filling me with warmth and power. I felt invincible.

Was this what it was like to use magic properly?

The humans looked at each other, as unused to the sensation as I with their limited innate magic barely noticeable in normal times, but Saint Silvestro's skull was a powerful amplifier.

Broad grins spread over our faces, a moment of indulgence before the dragon's roar sounded again, closer.

Still driven by Han's spell, it stumbled towards us through the burning wreckage of the abbey, smashing walls under its bulk.

My heart pounded like it wanted to get out of my chest, because if the dragon was here, that meant it no longer considered Fulgor a threat.

I strained my ears for any sound that my blue friend was alive but couldn't hear his deep voice. I spoke through our psychic connection and told him to hang on. There was no reply.

"Again!" I shouted, "Use everything you have."

We repeated the incantation as the dragon loomed over us, its fangs dripping with golden blood from my beloved Fulgor.

Anger and grief flared through me, churning my stomach, and burning my chest. My dragon scale necklace heated against my skin, lending whatever power it had to our chant.

This time, as we said its name, the dragon stumbled and shook its head. The film cleared from its eyes for an instant before its slitted pupils disappeared again.

I stepped forward, closer to the dragon, lifting the skull high, and repeated the spell with force.

Threads of invisible power shot from us, taking everything I had. Around me, the other women gasped as they felt it too. The skull absorbed all our magic and then shot it at the dragon in a haze of shimmering power.

The dragon stilled. Its golden eyes cleared, and I fancied there was a look of gratitude in them before they closed again, and it descended into sleep, collapsing among the remains of the abbey.

"Is it done?" asked the Mother Superior, panting hard from the exertion of using so much magic.

I swallowed and walked over to the sleeping form of the red dragon. Gently, I touched its snout. There was no reaction.

"I am so sorry," I whispered, my heart swelling with grief and what this poor creature had gone through against its will.

Shesalva appeared at my side. "It's over."

I stared up at her. "No…" I dashed over to where Fulgor lay. It wasn't over. I couldn't lose him.

Chapter 52

Fulgor lay sprawled in the dust near the wreckage of the abbey. One of his glorious wings had a gash through its thin webbing and his hot, golden blood dripped from several deep cuts to his side.

I hugged his snout, relishing the warm gusts of breath that wheezed from him.

Words failed me. I had no healing magic to save him, and any medical supplies the convent may have had lay hidden beneath the smoking rubble.

Shesalva knelt by my side. She shot me a strange look, before determination tensed her delicate jawline.

The elf placed one hand on Fulgor's sapphire blue scales, and her magic flowed through into him.

She sagged with exhaustion as she poured every ounce of healing power she had left into my friend, the dragon. Before my eyes, the cuts healed into fresh scars and his wing repaired itself, the thin flesh knitting itself into an ugly pattern.

"Thank you," croaked Fulgor in Draconic.

I placed my hand over hers. "Thank you," I repeated in Elvish. I meant it. She had helped us stop the red dragon, put herself in danger, and she had saved my friend. If I hadn't already given her my heart, I might have fallen in love with her again.

Shesalva gave me a tight nod. I let her work, admiring her magic and marvelling that she was here.

When she finally pulled her hand away, her skin was gaunt and there were bags under her eyes. It was the first time I had seen her as anything less than perfect – or maybe it was the first time I had allowed myself to see it, removed her from the pedestal I had placed her on and seen her as the elf she was.

Either way, I loved her. There was no running away from this. I was in love.

And she was here.

In the middle of rural Italy stood the person I had flown over a thousand miles to escape.

We didn't have time to talk because it was about then that flashing lights and sirens erupted around us. Someone had spotted the flames and called the fire brigade. With extreme efficiency, they doused the flames, so the nunnery was a steaming mess instead of a smoking one.

The Mother Superior ordered the firefighters and the nuns about, salvaging what they could from the wreckage. I hoped the books could be saved. I wanted to help but my legs stopped working and I stayed near my friend instead, lending him what comfort I could.

It was about then that the Italian equivalent of the Magic Liaison Office turned up to question us. Maybe the nuns' secret wasn't as well kept as they thought because the harpy in charge asked a lot of questions in rapid Italian.

I considered using my ruse of not understanding but one look from the harpy in charge reminded me of Agent Jones on a bad day. My instincts kicked in and I found myself giving her a debrief.

"Where is the skull now?" she asked, glaring at the rubble as if her gaze could pierce the debris and find the artefact.

I opened my mouth to tell her where I'd last seen in when Sister Theresa caught my eye. She winked and put her finger over her lips. Guess the nuns wanted to keep the dragon-raising skull of a saint quiet. I shrugged and mumbled that I didn't know.

The harpy – Agent Ricci – scowled, but the Mother Superior called her away to deal with Han who had regained consciousness and was now defending himself from an irate Sister Ursula. I breathed out a sigh of relief, not sure my training would have helped me stand up to a more thorough investigation.

The nuns all had silver space blankets around their shoulders and a group of nonnas from the nearest village had come over with mugs of warm liquid that smelled of coffee and alcohol. I drank deeply and managed to stand, the exhaustion replaced by mere weariness. If I closed my eyes, I could imagine we were at a bonfire instead of the site of such destruction.

Shesalva stood near me, following me as I checked on everyone, but staying silent, like a shadow.

"Shall we go for a walk?" My mouth moved ahead of my brain, but the tall elf nodded, and we strode away from the recovering dragon and the wreckage of the abbey.

Chapter 53

Shesalva was as beautiful as I remembered; tall, slender, with red-gold hair that hung down her back and shimmered in the remains of the late evening sunset. My heart clenched as I gaped up at the amazing elf, still clutching her bow. She was a goddess, able to kill or heal at her whim. And she was still here with me.

"What are you doing here?" I whispered, afraid I might break into pieces at her answer.

She moved with an awkward elegance, reached out to tuck a strand of my hair behind one ear, then stopped. "Saving Fulgor."

"No, I mean here. Why are you here? In Italy?"

"I couldn't get hold of you." She sighed and started pacing. "I was worried. You haven't posted online. One of your followers kept posting messages that grew more and more disturbing. I went to Fulgor, and we agreed we should make sure you were safe. I had to know you were safe…"

So many questions chased each other through my mind, but the one I ended up asking was, "How did you speak with a dragon?"

The elf blushed and looked at her feet. "I looked up your borrowing history at the library. I've been learning Draconic. I know how important it is to you. I wanted to surprise you. So…surprise." She gave me a weak smile.

My mouth fell open. Then I frowned as I thought back on my reading record. "Good job I didn't take out any racy books."

Shesalva laughed, a bright tinkle laced with magic. If I didn't know better, I'd have said she was casting some sort of enchantment on me because I wanted her. My battered heart longed for her, and I wanted to believe she was here for me, but I couldn't quite grasp at why. I swallowed. If we had any chance at starting over, I needed to be honest with her. "I don't understand. I thought you wanted to take a break."

"You are so wild…"

"Did you come all this way to insult me?" Anger flooded through me, driving all my resolutions of honesty and understanding away. I had given her space. I had left the dzraking country to give her space, and she followed me here to tell me that I had messed things up. I opened my mouth again, ready to let loose a tirade at the elf who broke my heart, but she stopped me with one word.

"Please."

I nodded, crossing my arms tight across my stomach as if that could protect me from her words when she broke my heart for a second time.

"I wanted to tell you before you left, but you were so angry."

I clamped my mouth shut. She had rejected me. Of course I was angry.

"You are a whirlwind through my life. You have shaken me to my core, and I made a great mistake. Because elves live so long, I thought I had time. We do not usually move so fast in our courtships. It was strange and scary for me…but when I thought I'd lost you…" Shesalva shuddered. "I knew for certain. You are the other half of my heart. I know you cannot forgive how I treated you, but if there is any way I can undo the hurt, I will."

She gripped both my hands in hers and met my gaze. "Aloora, you are the love of my life. I wish to spend the rest of my years with you. If you still want me, I will give everything to putting right the wrong I have done."

And my hurt and pain floated away on her speech. She loved me. And I loved her. I knew it in my heart and soul and head. This was what I wanted. Someone who accepted me for being me, someone who shared my love of books and knowledge, someone who would always support me and never want me to change.

"I understand if you do not want me any longer." Shesalva turned to walk away.

"Of course I want you!" I blurted out, my hand on her sleeve to stop her leaving me. She opened her mouth again. I pressed my finger to her lips to stop her from ruining the moment with more apologies. "Just kiss me."

Epilogue

I waited in the long queue just off stage in St David's Hall. I plucked at my long robes and rearranged them.

A steward repeated the instructions they'd already given us three times. "Speeches first. Then, when your name is called; walk across the stage, take your certificate, shake hands lightly, and walk to the other side and back to your seat. Any questions?"

There were no questions. There had been no questions the first two times either.

I rocked back and forth in my boots. The hall filled with anticipation and the low hum of noise stopped as the guest speaker and famous alumnus, elven popstar Cirian, stepped forward for his speech.

He brushed his perfect, long hair away from his face and gave the crowd a dazzling smile. His robes hung like they were custom made, and he looked comfortable in them. They were looser than traditional elven garb, and he wore them like he had chosen to instead of being forced to like the rest of us.

"Hello everyone." A cheer sounded in the room, and he smiled again, used to performing. "Usually, you'll find me in venues like this performing, but don't worry, I'm not going to sing today."

A forced laugh rippled across the crowd and a faint chorus of 'awwws' from the back of the room. Someone shouted, 'we love you Cirian'. He ignored that and carried on.

"Today we're all here for one reason; these fantastic people who have dedicated a good portion of their lives to completing their degrees.

"I got a lot out of my music degree at this very school and I'm not talking about the fancy certificate either." Another smattering of laughter. He had the crowd in the palm of his hand.

"Cardiff University is where I made some of my very best friends and where I learned about myself, who I was and what I could achieve. As I look out here today, I see a room full of potential and all I can say is; best of luck for the future and Caerdydd am Byth!"

A tremendous cheer sparked across the crowd at his use of Welsh, and my face split into a grin.

He waved away the cheers and returned to his seat. The Dean, an older woman with large glasses shaped like triangles, and a billowy robe stood and approached the microphone.

She coughed. "Thank you, Cirian, one of our biggest success stories here at Cardiff University." There was another round of cheers.

Someone pushed their way out of the queue and opened their robes, facing the stage to reveal their naked body. "Marry me, Cirian!" they shouted, their voice so husky I couldn't tell if they were a male or female flasher.

The Dean motioned to two security guards who escorted the crazed graduate out of the theatre.

"Well, after that, ahem, small interruption…let me say that I am so proud of our graduates here today. You have all worked so hard to get where you are, and I have no doubt that you will all move on to great things. Here at Cardiff University, we know that we only get to have you for a short amount of time, and we encourage you to explore ideas and challenge preconceived knowledge.

"We have a strong tradition of learning built on our values of institutional autonomy and freedom of enquiry to encourage creative curiosity.

"And I also note our tradition of building strong social and civic ties and the sense of social inclusion and giving back to the community that we engender here. I know many of you will stay local to Cardiff and continue to contribute to the thriving community and economy here in Wales.

"Our graduates go on to many things, from cutting edge research to industry and even more creative fields such as writing. I am proud to present you with these certificates as a token of what you have achieved with us. Ladies and Gentlemen…"

There was a pause as an aide stood and whispered in her ear. "…and everybody in between, please come and collect your degrees."

I rolled my eyes at the awkward words. It was a nice token to equality but could have been phrased better.

A deafening round of applause swept through the room as another aide called the first name.

The queue inched forward as each of us was called one by one to the stage. And then it was my turn.

I winced at my birth name – Aloora Neebly – there was a reason I used Dragonquest as my online handle – but the university was insistent on using legal names only.

I walked up on stage, feeling tiny under the glaring lights. The Dean passed me a rolled-up certificate and shook my hand so gently it was hard to know she'd even made contact with my palm.

This was it. The culmination of over a decade of work to finish my thesis; *Talking with dragons, a comprehensive study of cases and contextualism in Draconic.* And I wasn't going to let an anti-climactic handshake dull my pride.

I turned and smiled into the live stream camera, giving my supporters who tuned in a wave.

Up in the stands, a whoop and cries of 'Dragonquest' told me that was where Amethyst and Shesalva sat. I waved in their direction as I made my way offstage and to my allocated seat. Professor Maron – my liaison for the degree – winked at me as I sat down. He was in professorial black robes but sported a bowtie in his trademark tweed. I waved back, unable to wipe the grin from my face. I'd done it. I finally had my PhD. It felt like a chapter of my life – one I had kept open for far too long – had closed. And I was ready for my next chapter to begin.

With an efficiency that Agent Jones would envy, the ceremony ended, and we filed out, blinking at the sudden sunshine.

I hovered by the steps in the dull drizzle until Amethyst bounded out and scooped me up in a hug. "You were dzraking brilliant. Shame the speeches went on so long."

I laughed.

Shesalva kissed me. "Congratulations Dr Dragonquest."

I gave a mock bow before hugging her. "So, how are we celebrating?"

Amethyst tapped the side of her nose. "Follow me."

Frowning, I held my fiancée's – yes, fiancée! I didn't think I'd ever tire of saying that – hand, and we walked the short distance to The Goat. My heart sank. It might have been the oldest supernatural pub in Cardiff, but it wasn't an elegant location to celebrate the thirteen years I'd spent working on my doctorate. I'd expected a fancy meal at a restaurant or something, not a dirty pint served by a troll.

Shesalva sensed my lack of enthusiasm and squeezed my hand. "Don't worry," she whispered in Elvish.

"I am married to an elf, you know," Amethyst said.

"So did you understand Shesalva?" I asked.

"No," she shrugged.

I shook my head. Amethyst was many things; loyal, funny, a brilliant craftswoman, but a linguist she was not.

Just before we entered, a group of fresh graduates charged over. "Are you Princess Amethyst? You are, aren't you? Can we have your autograph?"

Their gazes raked over her like they wanted to steal part of her soul before they took in my gorgeous elf standing next to her. "Are you an elf princess, too?"

I stepped in front of my friend and the love of my life. Amethyst was too nice to say no, and it was about time I saved her – and my elven librarian – from something. "Sorry, she's busy." I glared at them until they left.

Amethyst laughed at my protectiveness and pushed open the heavy wooden door, complete with original studs hammered into the bars, and ushered me inside The Goat, ignoring the sign hung that declared it was closed for a private function.

As my eyes adjusted to the gloomy interior, I gasped. Silver streamers hung from every part of the ceiling covering the original Tudor beams, and a huge banner stretched across the back wall saying 'Congratulations'. Underneath it, a huge crochet dragon glowered at us.

I felt tears well up in my blue eyes as all my friends and colleagues gave a huge cheer.

Agent Jones strode over and shook my hand. "Glad you did it, Dragonquest. Don't overdo it." She clapped a hand on my shoulder. "You've got work tomorrow."

I smiled. Typical.

Dot jumped up and down next to her. "Don't mind her. What do you think of the decorations?"

"They're perfect."

"I knew it! Amethyst said the crochet dragons were too much, but I knew you'd love them. They'll look great in your house too; I made them fully posable."

I kept my smile fixed on my face. I had no idea how they could fit in our flat.

Marco came over and pulled me into a hug. "Congratulations!" He lowered his voice, "If those…things come in our flat even for one second, I will cut them into pieces and use them to stuff my new cushions."

"Don't worry, I'll sort it." Maybe I could convince Shesalva to store them in Breconia. We had talked about moving there together, but hadn't made formal plans. I was trying to take things slow for once and enjoy the now instead of rushing into the future.

Goat – the troll owner of the pub – poured me a 'Dragonquest' cocktail with an extra kick and I choked on the fiery drink, spitting out flames.

"Dwarven fire whisky. Amethyst insisted." He shrugged and poured another.

Amethyst came over, thrust Dafydd at Lorandir – her husband – and hugged me. "Congratulations again!"

"Thank you. This is perfect."

She beamed. "So, what's your plan now you're engaged?"

"Not sure. Shesalva doesn't want to give up her job in the library and I still have my job here in Cardiff, although Professor Maron offered me a field job in his department if I want it. We'll work something out."

As if saying his name had summoned him, the elven professor sauntered over. He had replaced his robes with a set made of tweed that fluttered down to the ground in thick drapes of fabric. "Congratulations, Aloora. I was a little worried, but you did it in the end."

"I was worried, too," I confessed.

"All good things to those who take the time."

I smiled at the elven proverb.

Amethyst nudged me in the ribs. "I'm glad you got your happy ending. She's perfect for you."

"I know."

"But if she breaks your heart again, I'll snap her like a twig."

I laughed and pulled my best friend into a hug. She was loyal to a fault.

Shesalva glided over. "My ears are burning."

"We were just talking about you."

"No. I had some of the fire whisky and I think my ears are actually on fire."

I checked – you couldn't be too careful with Dwarven spirits – and her gorgeous, pointed ears were red but not smoking.

"Come on, let's get you a glass of water and talk about where we're going to put the crochet dragons." I placed my arm around her slender waist and propelled her to the bar.

If you enjoyed reading this book, please leave a review on amazon, goodreads or bookbub. And you can read a bonus chapter showing the proposal at

https://books.gemmaclatworthy.com/Eat_Pray_Dragons_Bonus

Did you spot any typos? Let me know by dropping me an email at gemma@gemmaclatworthy.com

A Note from the Author

There are many interesting stories that I researched for this book, and I loved digging back into history and actually using some of my degree.

First, the nymph Vegoia – in my story, the ancestor of the Vegoia family – was part of Rome's founding story, in particular passing on both religious rites and laws to the first two kings of Rome.

Second, the jaculus – a winged serpent that launched itself from trees like a javelin – is mentioned by both Pliny and Lucan so I had to include one at the Vegoia's home.

Third, Saint Silvestro really was said to have tamed a dragon at the request of Constantine, the first Christian Emperor of Rome. Of course, in my story, he took the dragon out of Rome and enchanted it to sleep later.

The Abbey of Saint Silvestro is entirely fictitious as are the nuns who dwell there. The collective noun for a group of nuns is a convent or cloister, not a gaggle or holiness as Aloora guesses.

Fourth, yes there really is a section of a museum in Naples dedicated to erotic archaeological finds from the nearby Pompeii and Herculaneum. I visited it during a summer I spent in Italy when the bin strikes were on in fore. It's comforting to know we're not the only generation obsessed with sex.

A note on dragons; as far as I am aware, there are no dragons sleeping under any religious buildings in Italy…

Thank you

A special thank you to my amazing patrons: Emma Ward, Mark Canty and Bevan Clatworthy who always support me.

If you want to support Gemma, you can find her on www.patreon.com/G_Clatworthy for exclusive first reads of new stories.

You can also join her newsletter for at www.gemmaclatworthy.com for a free prequel to her Rise of Dragons series and a free short story based on one of the Omensford witches. You can follow Gemma on www.instagram.com/gemmaclatworthy, www.facebook.com/gemmaclatworthy or join the Facebook reader's group Gemma's book wyrms.

Other Books by G Clatworthy

Books in the Rise of the Dragons series:

Awakening

Solstice of Dragons

Equinox Betrayal

Darkest Deception

Attack on Avalon

Fated Bloodlines

Eat, Pray, Dragons

Books in the Omensford series (set in the Rise of the Dragons universe):

Bedsocks and Broomsticks

Cream Teas and Crystal Balls

Donkeys and Demons

Pumpkins and Popstars

Exes and Enchantments

Fae and Familiars

Gnomes and Necromancy

Books in the Saffron Vale series (a cozy fantasy series, part of the Cozy Vales universe):

A Colour to Dye For

Going for Guild

Commission Impossible

Short stories based on board games:

Ghostel

Haunticulture

Children's Books

The Child Who series:

The Girl Who Lost Her Listening Ears

The Boy Who Lost His Listening Ears

The Girl Who Dreamed of Sleep

The Boy Who Dreamed of Sleep

Nanny Pastry series:

Nanny Pastry and the Nimble Ninjabread Man

Other books:

Coronavirus in the words of children

About the Author

Gemma started writing during the 2020 lockdown and loves fantasy fiction and dragons in particular. She lives in Wiltshire with her family and two cats and also enjoys crafts of all kinds. You can see all her writing on www.patreon.com/G_Clatworthy. Join the conversation at Gemma's book wyrms readers' group on Facebook.

She also writes children's books. You can find out more on her website www.gemmaclatworthy.com or follow her on Instagram (www.instagram.com/gemmaclatworthy) or Facebook (www.facebook.com/gemmaclatworthy).